MAIA *and* ICARUS

by

JAMES A. PEREZ

BARROW COURT BOOKS

HUNTINGTON, NEW YORK

For M., whose smile still melts my heart

For J., one of the bravest people I've ever known

Text copyright © 2013 by James A. Perez

Cover and chapter heading illustrations
by Peter Prabowo copyright © 2013 by Barrow Court Books

For information regarding permission, write to:
Barrow Court Books, 55 Gerard Street #1219
Huntington, New York, 11743

Art directed and designed by Michael Ebert.

ISBN 978-0-9891762-2-4

CONTENTS

The world is too much with us; late and soon,
Getting and spending, we lay waste our powers;
Little we see in Nature that is ours;
We have given our hearts away, a sordid boon!
This Sea that bares her bosom to the moon;
The winds that will be howling at all hours,
And are up-gathered now like sleeping flowers,
For this, for everything, we are out of tune;
It moves us not.—Great God! I'd rather be
A pagan suckled in a creed outworn;
So might I, standing on this pleasant lea,
Have glimpses that would make me less forlorn;
Have sight of Proteus rising from the sea;
Or hear old Triton blow his wreathèd horn.

William Wordsworth
(1770–1850)

MAIA *and* ICARUS

THERE IS STILL TIME

THE SEA GOD TOYED with the idea of drowning the noisy children playing in the surf. *A whirlpool will quiet them.*

As tempting as the thought was, the sea god recalled the mandate he'd been given. "You are to observe, and not to interfere," he'd been instructed. "Walk amongst them if you must, but do not interfere."

The sea god rolled listlessly beneath the cloudy sea. He hadn't ventured this far from home for a very long time, and the journey had hardly been a pleasant one. Even now, the sea god bristled at the toxic chemicals and plastic trash contaminating the water. *They all deserve drowning for bringing such poisons into this realm.*

The sea god brought his attention back to the children playing. *None show the mark.*

Swimming farther out into the harbor, the sea god considered his options. *There is still time.*

The sea god stopped in the middle of the harbor and allowed himself to drift upward. Gently breaking the surface, the sea god looked toward the cliffs that gave this place its name.

Where are you, child of two worlds?

CHAPTER 1

THE OBJECT IN THE HARBOR

MAIA PETERSON RUSHED HOME from school, a broad smile reflecting her excitement. She'd reached the end of an unremarkable year in seventh grade, and she had one final exam before her. After tomorrow morning, Maia would have the entire summer to herself. As she quickened her pace, thoughts of cool summer evenings spent strumming her guitar on her front porch filled Maia's head.

In her haste, Maia barely acknowledged the group of boys from her class skateboarding on the steps of the Sea Cliff Village Library. That is, until one of the boys, having failed to complete an ill-conceived stunt, slipped off his skateboard and sent it sailing toward Maia. She jumped out of the way and turned to glare at the boys, who were laughing at their fallen friend as he lay on the ground nursing a bruised ankle. Maia shook her head. Boys could be so stupid.

Maia had turned thirteen in May, and she felt every bit the awkward teenager. She thought that her dark brown hair was too bushy, her face too oily, and her body parts too mismatched. She excelled at sports – lacrosse being her best – and she was (discreetly) proud of being such a good athlete, especially since she could more than challenge some boys twice her size. While she played the flute in the band at school, Maia was also an exceptional guitar player. And though she was a fair student, Maia would say there wasn't much else she liked about being in middle school other than sports and music.

Maia rushed past Sea Cliff Memorial Park with its sweeping view of the harbor. As usual, Maia failed to be taken in by the seaside charm of her small village. Sea Cliff's inviting beaches and towering Victorian-style homes often impressed visitors to the north shore of Long Island, but Maia gave these things little thought as she rounded the corner of her block. She was surprised to see her mother closing the front door of their modest ranch-style house and walking to her car. Mrs. Peterson was wearing cranberry-colored nursing scrubs and a white, hooded sweatshirt.

"Mom!" Maia called out. "Why are you dressed for work?"

Mrs. Peterson's shoulders dropped as she turned to face her daughter. "Maia, please don't start with me. You knew there was a chance I'd get called for overtime today." As she rifled through her handbag for her car keys, her mother asked, "How was your English final?"

Maia ignored the question and walked toward her mother, letting her backpack slide off her shoulder and fall to the ground. "But you said we could go to the music store. I need new picks and—"

"No, what you need is to study," interrupted her mother. She opened the car door and placed her handbag inside. "Do you remember what your social studies teacher told me? If you don't do well on the final, you could end up with a 'C' or worse for the year."

Failing to meet her daughter's eyes, Mrs. Peterson sighed. "Maia, I can't turn down overtime when the hospital calls. You know that. I'll make it up to you this weekend, okay?"

Maia stood in the driveway with her arms crossed.

"Grandpa is asleep on the couch," her mother continued, "and I left your dinner in the fridge. I should be home by midnight."

Her mother approached Maia to give her a kiss, but Maia turned her back to her. Sighing again, Mrs. Peterson got in her car and pulled away. Maia quietly stared at a weed growing in a crack in the cement until her mother was gone.

When Maia looked up at her house, she noticed an open bucket of paint next to an ashtray on the railing of the front porch. Her grandfather had been working to fulfill his promise to finish repainting the porch before school ended. Maia gave a slight head-shake. A little paint was hardly going to make a difference.

Maia dragged her backpack as she walked up the path to her front door. Entering the house, she heard her grandfather snoring in the living room. Maia tossed her backpack onto the dining room table and went into the kitchen to get a bottle of iced tea and a bag of pretzels. She noticed a stack of mail in a basket on the kitchen counter. On top of all the bills and catalogs was a letter with a foreign stamp addressed to her mother. Maia turned the envelope over but there was no return address. She tossed the letter back into the basket and walked into the dining room.

Maia emptied the contents of her backpack onto the dining room table and started to leaf through her social studies notebook. She did her best to ignore her grandfather's snoring, but after twenty minutes she no longer could. After stuffing her books into her backpack, Maia scrawled a note on a napkin on the kitchen counter explaining to her grandfather that she'd gone to the library to study.

As she approached the front door, Maia hoped that the skater boys had moved on to a less intrusive place. Her grandfather stirred on the couch, and Maia tiptoed past so as not to wake him. Though she loved him dearly, Maia wasn't in the mood to be questioned about her English final even though she knew her grandfather would want to hear every detail. It was as though everything she said fascinated him. The only thing Grandpa loved as much as her "stories" was a good cigar.

Maia passed Memorial Park again. This time, her attention was caught. Looking out at the harbor, she thought she saw something break the surface of the water. Maia was reminded of a poem she'd had to analyze on her English final – it included a line about someone rising from the sea. Before she could think about it any further, the object in the harbor vanished just as quickly as it had appeared. Maia shrugged and turned onto Sea Cliff Avenue, the main street of the village.

It had been years since she needed to hold her mother's hand when she walked through town. Though her backpack felt heavier than the first time her mother had kissed her on the cheek and told her to be home in time for dinner, little else in her world had changed. Maia had lived in Sea Cliff for as long as she could remember. Her mother, a pediatric nurse, had been born in the town, in the same house that Maia and her mother now lived in with her grandfather.

Maia's grandmother had died when Maia was five years old. A year later, her grandfather was hurt while doing construction work, leaving it to Maia's mother to make sure the family didn't lose their home. Compared to some of the other houses in town, the Peterson home was rather small – something Maia minded only when it was pointed out to her.

As she approached the library, Maia was grateful that the steps were now empty. Inside the library, it was cool and quiet, unlike at home, and after saying hello to the librarian, Maia settled down to study.

The library was one of Maia's favorite retreats since she was a little girl, even if reading wasn't as much fun as strumming her guitar or chasing a lacrosse ball. Still, the library was a comfortable fit, and Maia smiled as she remembered when her mother signed her up in kindergarten for "popcorn and picture books." She spent a lot of Saturday mornings sitting in her mother's lap reading about courageous farm animals and gluttonous caterpillars. As much as she welcomed the memory, Maia's mood soured as she struggled to remember the last time she'd been able to spend time alone with her mother. It had been a very long while.

Maia flipped through her social studies notebook, trying to remember which of the battles in the American Revolutionary War her teacher had told her to memorize. Boredom setting in, she looked around the library for distraction. Except for the librarian, there appeared to be only one other person there – a tall, lanky boy with glasses whom Maia recognized from school. He was a year older, and by the expression on his face he appeared to be enjoying studying for finals as much as Maia was.

Just as she thought she remembered his name, the boy lifted his head. He raised his eyebrows and offered a shy smile when he noticed Maia looking in his direction. Maia quickly returned her attention to her notebook, embarrassed to have been caught looking at him. But she raised her head again when she heard a voice coming from the front entrance.

"What a surprise to find you here!" said a girl in a pink tank top, also a year older than Maia. Surprise hardly appeared to be the look on her face, Maia thought. The same could be said for the two girls with her. Smirking, the girls strolled over to the boy. It was clear to Maia that he wasn't as excited to see them as they were by the prospect of having some fun at his expense.

"So, do you, like, live at the library?" the girl in pink asked, causing one of her two friends to laugh out loud.

"You're here too," the boy mumbled.

"Yeah, but, duh, only because it's raining out," she answered.

Maia turned and looked out the window. It had started to rain, which was surprising since there hadn't been a cloud in the sky when she walked into the library. Maia looked back at the other table where the girls continued to taunt the boy.

"Girls, if you're going to stay, you'll have to lower your voices," said the librarian, as she emerged from behind a bookcase.

"Oh, let's just get out of here," one of the other girls said, making a face. "Have fun!" the girl in pink added.

Maia watched them walk toward the entrance. Just before exiting, one of the girls looked at Maia and waved. Maia turned to the boy to give him a sympathetic smile, but he was too busy shoving his books into his backpack to see her. Without a word, he stormed out of the library. Maia watched as the boy passed outside the window, then looked back to the table he'd been sitting at just a few minutes ago. Maia frowned. Girls could be stupid too.

After two hours of studying, Maia's stomach was grumbling and she remembered the dinner her mother had left for her in the refrigerator at home. She packed up her books, waved goodbye to the librarian, and went out to the street. Thankful the rain had stopped, Maia headed home, careful to avoid the puddles on the sidewalk.

As she reached the corner of the block, a fire truck sped past, its siren blaring. Just a minute later, another fire truck passed, followed by an ambulance. They were all headed in the direction of her house. Maia felt a sickening pang in her stomach, not from hunger, but from a sense that something was wrong at home. She broke into a run, slowed only by the weight of her backpack as it thumped against her with each step. Maia panted as she rounded the corner of her block. Between the emergency vehicles and a crowd that had gathered, she could barely see her house – it was on fire!

"No!" Maia cried. "Grandpa!"

Maia ran to the house, pushing her way through the crowd, but was prevented from getting too close when someone grasped her arm. It was Mrs. Tuttle, her next-door neighbor.

"Let me go!"

"Maia, please stop!" begged Mrs. Tuttle. "They have your grandfather in the ambulance. He managed to get out, but he collapsed on the lawn." Mrs. Tuttle held Maia's hands in hers. "I called your mother. She's on her way."

"But what about our house?" Maia asked, her voice trembling. "How bad is it?"

"I don't know, dear," said Mrs. Tuttle. "They're putting the fire out very quickly. Thank goodness you weren't home!"

Maia looked at her house. She couldn't tell how badly it was damaged. The front bay window was smashed and there were several dark spots on the roof. Maia looked around for the ambulance. Was Grandpa going to be okay?

"Maia!" a voice shrieked, through the din of the crowd. Maia turned to see her mother running to her.

"Mom!"

"Maia! Oh, baby!" cried her mother, as she gripped Maia in her arms. "Are you okay? What happened? Where's Grandpa?"

"Grandpa's in the ambulance. Mom, I don't know what happened! I went to the library to study."

Her mother leaned in and kissed Maia on the cheek, and then hurried over to the ambulance. Maia wanted to go with her but Mrs. Tuttle told her to stay by her side. A few minutes later, her mother called out to Maia.

"I'm going in the ambulance with Grandpa. Mrs. Tuttle, can Maia stay with you?"

"Of course, dear," answered Mrs. Tuttle, placing her hand on Maia's shoulder.

Helplessly, Maia watched her mother climb into the back of the ambulance. It wasn't until the ambulance had sped away that Maia realized she was holding Mrs. Tuttle's hand.

CHAPTER 2

A WHOLE OTHER WORLD

IT WAS AFTER MIDNIGHT when Maia was awoken by voices coming from Mrs. Tuttle's kitchen. She squinted as she looked around the room. Maia had fallen asleep on the couch in the small den just off the kitchen. She sat up and listened for her mother's voice.

"Is Maia asleep?" she heard her mother ask.

"Yes, dear," answered Mrs. Tuttle. "The poor girl was exhausted. She didn't say much, but I think I heard her crying."

Maia huffed. Why did Mrs. Tuttle have to say that? The last thing she ever wanted to let her mother know, even when Maia was a small girl, was when she was upset. It was difficult enough that her mother worked as many hours as she did to provide for her and Grandpa. Maia didn't want to add to her burden. Given what had occurred today, Maia was even more resolved to keep her feelings from her mother. After a few moments, she stood and approached the door leading to the kitchen.

"How is your father?" Mrs. Tuttle asked.

Maia stopped to listen to what her mother said about her grandfather's condition, knowing that she would probably be honest with Mrs. Tuttle.

"He's in an induced coma with burns on his arms and chest. The doctors are going to keep him unconscious for a few days, but they think in time he'll be alright," Mrs. Peterson recounted.

Maia was relieved. She knew from experience that her mother wouldn't repeat something a doctor had said unless she believed it.

"They think he fell asleep smoking," her mother continued. "If he wasn't already in the hospital, I'd do something to put him there. If Maia had been home, in her room with the music on... "

Maia heard her mother sobbing.

"It's okay, dear. Maia is fine," said Mrs. Tuttle.

Maia's lip quivered. She reached for the handle of the door but hesitated when she heard her mother raise her voice.

"No! No, she's not fine! How could she be fine? Not with our life the way it is. This isn't what I wanted. It's not what I ever wanted. I'd gotten off Long Island, but I came back because of them." Her mother paused. "I left a whole other world to come back here. And what now? I get to take care of another ailing parent?"

Maia was shocked to hear her mother speak to Mrs. Tuttle in that way. And she'd certainly never heard her mother talk about some "other world." Unsure whether she should let her mother know she was awake, Maia kept her hand on the door handle until she heard her mother sigh, which was always a sign that she was calming down.

"My dear," began Mrs. Tuttle, "your parents knew you weren't happy coming home after your mother had her stroke, but your father couldn't take care of her by himself. And they missed you so terribly. It always felt like a blessing in disguise. They had their only daughter back and a beautiful granddaughter as well. I know you must have loved your life in Italy, but surely—"

"Greece," Maia's mother interrupted. "We lived in Greece."

"Oh, I'm sorry, dear. Your mother always said Italy."

"I know. Even before the stroke she couldn't tell the two apart. I asked them to come for a visit after Maia was born. My mother said she might, but that my father probably wouldn't because he really didn't like Italian food."

Maia heard her mother and Mrs. Tuttle share a soft laugh.

"I'm sure my mother told you that I never felt like I belonged here. Maybe I didn't look or act the right way. I used to sit on a bench in Memorial Park and look out at the water, thinking of all the places I could go. It was a miracle that my parents let me go to college in the city. It was an even bigger miracle that they didn't try to stop me from going to Europe the summer after graduation. It was the happiest I'd ever been. Spain, France, Italy – they were more wonderful than I'd envisioned. Greece wasn't even a place I'd thought about visiting. But when my plans to go to Switzerland fell through, I found myself on a ferry from Bari to Patras."

Maia could barely breathe. She dared not move for fear that her mother would stop talking, even if she couldn't believe what her mother was saying. As far as Maia knew, her mother had never left Long Island, let alone the United States.

"I was in Athens. I hadn't taken a proper shower in weeks, and I probably looked like I was homeless. For the life of me, I couldn't find a youth hostel. I was staring up at the Acropolis when he tapped me on the shoulder. He asked me if I needed help. The first thing I noticed was his smile. His English was bad and my Greek was even worse, but somehow we managed to strike up a conversation.

"I never made it to a youth hostel. Instead, he drove me on the back of his motorcycle to Cape Sounion, outside of Athens. It was like being in one of those old black-and-white movies my mother loved. Under the stars, on a beach overlooked by the Temple of Poseidon, I fell in love. A few days later I wrote my parents that I wasn't coming home, and a month later, I was married. Maia was born the year after. I thought I had everything I ever hoped for."

Maia heard her mother stifle a sob.

"And then one day, when Maia was barely a year old, he disappeared. He left without saying anything. At first, his family told me not to worry because he'd done this before. They insisted that he would never leave Maia and me. But, after a few weeks, even they couldn't hide their concern, especially his mother.

"Once, I overheard a conversation between her and one of his brothers – something about a journey or quest. Even though I spoke Greek very well by then, there were still some things I didn't understand. When I asked them about it, they pretended not to know what I was talking about. I got angry, and I told them I knew they were all keeping something from me. His mother cried and asked that I be patient. She insisted he would return. The next morning, the phone call came from my father telling me that my mother was sick. I felt there was nothing left for me in Greece, so I went home. Twelve years later, here I am."

Maia struggled to accept what her mother was saying. Though she didn't want to believe that she'd been lied to for years about her father, Maia had little proof otherwise. She strained to remember the rare occasions when her father had ever been mentioned. Maia had been led to think that her parents knew each other for a very short period of time and that her father had died before she was born. Maia felt her throat go dry, and she took several deep breaths. Her sense of uneasiness grew with each exhalation.

After a few moments of silence, Maia heard Mrs. Tuttle ask, "And that was it, dear? You never heard from him again?"

"No, and as far as I know, neither has his family. I get a letter from his mother every so often, one today in fact, asking me to come back, to let them see Maia, but I'm not interested. I don't even bother to read the letters anymore. That part of my life is over." After a pause, she continued. "I'm so sorry about raising my voice before, especially with all you've done. I can't thank you enough for letting us stay with you."

"Of course, dear. Maia can stay in the den, and you have the spare bedroom upstairs," said Mrs. Tuttle. "You know, dear, your mother cried when you wrote them that you were staying in Europe. At first, I thought it was because she was going to miss you so. But then she told me she wasn't sad. She was happy – happy that you'd found what you'd always wanted, something you couldn't find here." Mrs. Tuttle paused. "I don't think she would've wanted you to stay after she passed on."

"What are you saying?"

"I'm saying that taking Maia to Greece may be something... that would please both of her grandmothers," offered Mrs. Tuttle.

"I should check on Maia. Good night, Mrs. Tuttle, and again, thank you."

Maia dove facedown onto the couch. She pretended to be asleep when her mother came in and kissed her on the side of her forehead. After her mother left the room, Maia turned onto her back and stared up at the ceiling. There was so much for Maia to take in. She was born in Greece, and she had a grandmother who wanted her to visit.

Different images flashed through her mind – the letter she'd seen in the basket, her grandfather lying in a hospital bed, and her mother as a girl, sitting on a bench in Memorial Park. One last image was fuzzy, but much clearer than it had ever been – her father, alive, Maia hoped, and as eager to see her as she was to see him.

CHAPTER 3

THE LETTER WITH THE FOREIGN STAMP

WITH SCHOOL OVER and her mother always at the hospital, either working or visiting her grandfather, Maia spent most of July at the library. She devoured every book she could find on Greece. Back at Mrs. Tuttle's house, her guitar, which had survived the fire unscathed, sat untouched. Instead of spending her summer writing music, Maia did little else but think about the country where she'd been born and plot how to convince her mother to take her there.

One humid afternoon, after leaving the library, Maia stopped and sat on a bench in Memorial Park. She thought of her mother as a young girl, quite possibly sitting on the same bench, dreaming of a world beyond this one. Until a few weeks ago, Maia wouldn't have thought that she could feel the same way her mother had. True, she missed having a father sometimes, and she wished that she'd had more time with her grandmother. But before she discovered that her life had begun in a very distant place, she thought no more of leaving her home town than she did of trying out for cheerleading.

Maia found it difficult to reconcile herself to the idea that her mother could have been so unhappy. Maybe it was because her mother had always tried to make the best of every situation, even now with her grandfather in the hospital. Maia shook her head. There had to be a way to put things right. She needed to return to Greece as much for her mother as for herself.

As Maia rehearsed what to say to her mother, she spied a group of teenagers from the yacht club learning to operate daysailers out in the harbor. The water was rougher than usual, and it looked as if some of the teenagers were having a tough time controlling their boats. Then beyond the sailboats, she saw something else. For a moment, it appeared as though a man with a long, white beard was rising out of the water watching her. And then he was gone. Maia rubbed her eyes. She must have been reading too many books on Greek mythology. Maia grabbed her backpack to head home. As she stood and turned her back to the water, she heard what sounded like the loud blast of a trumpet echoing through the harbor.

A woman walking a black miniature poodle through the park stopped and stared at Maia, as if she expected to find her holding a large brass instrument in her hands. Maia, also puzzled about the origin of the trumpet blast, turned and looked back to the harbor. The teenagers in the sailboats were still there, but the water was now calm. Maia wondered if both her eyes and her ears were playing tricks on her, and came to the conclusion that she probably needed a good night's sleep. She left the park, the small dog barking wildly in her wake.

Maia's feet dragged as she approached her block. The past few weeks at Mrs. Tuttle's house hadn't been terrible, but she longed for time alone with her mother. Mrs. Tuttle's daughter spent the beginning of every summer in Sea Cliff with her husband and their two children, and this July was no different. With all of them feeling crowded, Maia's mother told Mrs. Tuttle that she and Maia would stay in a hotel, but Mrs. Tuttle wouldn't hear of it. Maia wished they had gone to a hotel, even though she knew it was an expense they really couldn't afford.

Maia passed her house, its boarded-up front window a reminder of that frightening afternoon. The fire destroyed most of the living and dining rooms, but the rest of the house was still in fair shape. Maia hadn't been able to talk to her mother much about when repairs would begin, but she understood it had something to do with waiting for insurance money. Though they were now both sharing the den at Mrs. Tuttle's house, she barely saw her mother. But tonight they were supposed to have dinner together after visiting her grandfather in the hospital. Maia wondered if this evening would be the right time to bring up the conversation she'd overheard between her mother and Mrs. Tuttle. The thought of doing so made her very uneasy. Maia had no idea where to start, and she was afraid she'd blurt out the wrong thing and make her mother sad or angry, or both.

"Hello, dear," called Mrs. Tuttle from the porch of her house. "How was the library?"

Mrs. Tuttle was holding her four-year-old granddaughter Molly on her lap, while Molly's twin brother Phillip was kicking a soccer ball on the front lawn.

"Fine," Maia replied. "Did my mother call?"

"Yes, she did. She'll be home in about an hour to pick you up."

"Did she say anything about Grandpa?" Maia asked.

"I'm afraid there's no change, dear. He still hasn't woken up."

Maia looked down at her feet to avoid Mrs. Tuttle's eyes. She felt guilty for how she'd been spending her days. As much as the prospect of traveling to Greece excited her, she hated the thought of her grandfather lying in a hospital bed with little improvement since the day of the fire. Maia looked at her house again and reminded herself how lucky she'd been.

"I was thinking of bringing the twins down to the playground. Would you like to come?" Mrs. Tuttle asked, as Molly climbed off her lap and joined her brother on the lawn.

Maia's face brightened. She knew Mrs. Tuttle's daughter and son-in-law were in New York City to see a Broadway show, and she prized the prospect of being alone in the house.

"That's okay. I think I'm going to play my guitar for a while," Maia lied.

"Okay, dear. If I'm not back before you leave, give your grandfather my best."

"I will," answered Maia, as Mrs. Tuttle took the twins by their hands. At Mrs. Tuttle's urging, Molly and Phillip waved goodbye as they walked down the block with their grandmother. Maia waited until they'd rounded the corner to enter Mrs. Tuttle's house. Her mother had brought several boxes over from their house a few days before – she'd left them in Mrs. Tuttle's basement. Maia hoped that one of those boxes contained the basket from the kitchen in which her mother kept the mail. Bounding down the basement stairs, Maia tore open the first box, only to find several photo albums and books. In the second box, Maia found what she was seeking. There, under a stack of papers from the hospital, was the basket.

The letter with the foreign stamp was still unopened. Maia debated what to do next. In the movies, people always used steam to open letters. She pictured the teakettle on Mrs. Tuttle's stove. But before she could plan her next step, Maia heard footsteps upstairs. Mrs. Tuttle must have forgotten something. Maia stood still, hoping Mrs. Tuttle would take what she needed and leave, but after a few tense moments her mother's voice called out for her.

"Maia, where are you?"

Maia rushed to close the boxes. She stuffed the letter in her back pocket.

"I'm downstairs," Maia yelled. "I'll be right up."

Slowly, Maia climbed the stairs. The wooden steps creaked ominously. This wasn't going to end well.

"What were you doing down there?" her mother asked.

"What are you doing home so early?" Maia asked in return, ignoring her mother's question as she stepped into the kitchen. "Mrs. Tuttle said you wouldn't be home for an hour."

"No, I wanted us to leave here in an hour. I've been at work since six in the morning. I need to shower and get ready before we go visit Grandpa," her mother said. "Maia, I asked you what were you doing down there."

Maia considered lying, but it was something that rarely worked when it came to her mother. The clock in Mrs. Tuttle's living room sounded five short chimes, allowing Maia a few precious moments to plan an escape from her mother's unblinking eyes. Her stare seemed capable, if necessary, of drilling a hole in Maia's forehead to get an answer.

"I was looking for this," she replied, fearful but nonetheless excited.

Maia reached into her back pocket and pulled out the letter.

Her mother clapped her hand to her mouth. She stared at the letter for what seemed like an eternity. Now it was Maia who refused to blink.

At long last, her mother said, "I think we should go for a walk."

CHAPTER 4

IN THE PARK

MAIA AND HER MOTHER sat on a bench in Memorial Park, an invisible barrier drawn between them. The harbor had emptied and the park had long since grown quiet. For the first time in weeks, they were truly alone.

They hadn't spoken since leaving Mrs. Tuttle's house, and though Maia had so many questions she wanted to ask, it was her mother who spoke first. "I wish you hadn't gone looking for that letter, Maia," she began.

Maia thought she would explode. "Mom!" she shouted. "Don't tell me you're going to yell at me when—"

"Who's the one yelling, Maia?" her mother interrupted, as she looked around the park to make sure no one had entered. Finally, she fixed her eyes on her daughter. "Let me finish," she said.

Calmed by the hope that perhaps her mother was going to reveal something important, Maia allowed her to continue. "Sorry," she mumbled. "I didn't mean to yell."

"As I was saying, I wish you hadn't gone looking for that letter because nothing good can come from it, especially not with Grandpa in the hospital."

"Mom, I heard you talking to Mrs. Tuttle the night of the fire. That letter is from my grandmother – a grandmother you never told me about." Maia stopped and picked at her fingers. "Just like you never told me the truth about my father."

Her mother shook her head. "Maia, if you heard everything I told Mrs. Tuttle that night, then you know there's a very good reason I never told you the truth." She paused. "How was I supposed to tell you that your father left us when you were just a baby? I didn't want to lie to you, but I didn't see that I had much of a choice. It was bad enough I had to live with your father's disappearance... and his broken promises."

Her mother's voice cracked before she could continue. She closed her eyes and bit her bottom lip. Maia looked at her mother with a mix of frustration and sympathy. It was becoming difficult to remain angry with her. As much as Maia wanted answers, it was clear that her mother couldn't provide them without reliving what was still a very painful time in her life. She sat next to her mother in silence for several minutes.

A breeze came up from the harbor and gently swayed the trees in the park. Two squirrels comically chased each other around a tree before disappearing into a bush. Maia's mother made an effort to smile as she dabbed at the corners of her eyes with a tissue from her handbag. Maia reached over and took her mother's free hand.

"I'm sorry, Maia. I haven't cried about your father in a very long time."

Leaning into her mother, Maia asked, "What was he like?"

"Oh, Maia," her mother answered with a breath it seemed she'd been holding in for twelve years. "He was crazy. Your father had to have been absolutely crazy to not want to watch you grow into the amazing person you are." Lovingly, she stroked Maia's bushy hair as a tear rolled down her cheek.

Maia straightened up. "Mom, I really want to know."

Her mother turned toward the harbor, an unsure look on her face. After a few seconds, she started to speak, almost in a whisper.

"When I first met your father, he swept me off my feet. He was funny and sweet, and he could talk me into doing just about anything, including staying in Greece."

Her mother grabbed Maia's chin and squeezed it the way her grandfather often would. "He had a smile just like yours," she continued. "When your father smiled, my heart skipped a beat. He had a way of making everything feel so light and easy."

Her mother paused, and from the pained expression on her face, Maia thought she might start crying again. When she spoke, it was with even greater difficulty. "But then other times, it was like he had the weight of the world on his shoulders. He was so different with his family. He would argue with his brothers whenever they were together. When I asked him why, he would always say it was an old family argument, and I shouldn't worry. Besides, it wasn't long before we had something more important to think about."

Her mother looked into Maia's eyes. "Your father was so happy when you were born. He was the one who chose your name. He used to call you his 'little star.' He said you were destined to shine down on the whole world. I wish he could see you now."

Her mother turned and faced the harbor again. "Maia, I'm so sorry you found out this way. I know I should've told you years ago, but there was never a right time, if such a thing exists."

For several minutes, Maia and her mother remained silent, each lost in their thoughts. An endless stream of questions flowed through Maia's mind. Why didn't her grandparents ever say anything? Did anyone else know? Was there more her mother was keeping from her? At that moment, however, none of Maia's questions mattered as much as wanting to tell her mother the secret she in turn was keeping from her.

"Mom, I want to go to Greece."

CHAPTER 5

THE BOOK OF GREEK MYTHS

THE AIRPORT IN ATHENS didn't appear to be much different than the one Maia had departed from in New York City. The people generally looked the same, even if she couldn't understand what they were saying. Some of the stores were also the same, though shopping was the last thing Maia had on her mind. As she made her way through the terminal, Maia stopped to soak in the moment. After twelve years, she was in Greece again.

What a long journey it had been, and not merely the ten-hour flight from New York City to Athens. After talking with her mother in Memorial Park, Maia never thought that she would be boarding an airplane to Greece two weeks later. Her mother's initial reaction had been a firm "No." There was no way she would allow Maia to travel to Greece, especially on her own. With her grandfather in the hospital, Maia's mother wasn't about to make a trans-Atlantic journey with her any time soon.

Refusing to give up hope, Maia persuaded her mother to do something she hadn't done in several years. She agreed to open the letter from Maia's grandmother in Greece. Though she wouldn't read it to Maia, after she finished with the letter, Maia's mother looked at her tearfully and said, "Maybe."

Maia knew it was best to say as little as possible. She occupied herself looking after Mrs. Tuttle's grandchildren or stealing away to the library to continue her private study of Greece. Each night, her mother would pick her up to go to the hospital to visit her grandfather. Regrettably, his condition hadn't improved. Maia wouldn't speak much in the car, and her mother was usually too tired from work for conversation. At the hospital, they would take turns reading to Grandpa, sometimes from the local newspaper but usually from an old detective novel he loved.

On the fourth night after Maia's talk in the park with her mother, the detective novel was missing from its usual place on her grandfather's side table. Maia's mother left the room to ask the nurse on duty if she'd seen it. A few minutes later, she returned to tell Maia that no one at the nurse's station had seen the book and she was going downstairs to buy a newspaper. She kissed Maia on the forehead before disappearing into the hallway.

Maia pulled a chair up next to her grandfather's bed. He hadn't been shaved for several days, and Maia wondered how he would look with a long, white beard. The mental picture of a bearded Grandpa reminded her of the cover of a book of Greek myths she'd taken out of the library that afternoon that she was carrying in her backpack. Reluctant to bring up anything related to Greece when her mother was around, Maia thought it would be okay to take a glance with her out of the room.

Maia reached into her backpack and pulled out the book. On the cover was a painting of Poseidon, the Greek god of the sea. She held the book up next to her grandfather, and, failing to see a resemblance, was about to put it away when her grandfather stirred and let out a soft moan.

"Grandpa?"

For weeks, her grandfather had shown no signs of response. Maia's heart raced. Should she stay or go to find her mother? Grandpa stirred again. His lips moved as if he was trying to form words. Maia waited to see if he would speak. After some time, a single word came forth from his lips.

"Book."

"Book!" Maia repeated in disbelief. "Grandpa, your book is missing. We looked but—"

"Book," her grandfather whispered again.

"My god," said Maia, "what am I supposed to do?" She stood up, causing the book of Greek myths to slide off her lap.

"Oh!" Maia exclaimed. "Grandpa, I can read to you from this until Mom comes back with the newspaper." Maia leafed through the book, settling on a story about the first Olympic Games.

"Like so many tales of ancient Greece, the first Olympic Games are shrouded in mystery and myth," Maia began.

She paused after every few words to glance up at her grandfather, but he showed no reaction. Maia finished the story in no time at all.

"Grandpa, do you want me to read another one?" She flipped through the pages of the book, pausing to look at a picture of two men with wings. Shaking her head, Maia kept turning the pages until she found a story she thought Grandpa would enjoy.

"This one is about Heracles." Maia began to read, watching her grandfather for any sign of movement. She'd just about finished the story when her mother returned, newspaper in hand.

"I'm sorry that took me so long, but I ran into one of the nurses I work with in—"

"Mom, Grandpa spoke! He said, 'book'!"

Her mother stood in the doorway, a puzzling look on her face. Maia thought she didn't believe her.

"I told him we couldn't find his book, so I took this from my backpack and started reading," Maia said.

Her mother barely glanced at the book in Maia's hands. She moved to Grandpa's side and ran her hand over his forehead. "Dad, can you hear me? Say something, please!"

Maia and her mother stared breathlessly at her grandfather. After a few seconds, he stirred again. As her mother gasped, Maia gave a soft cry of joy.

Grandpa's lips began to move.

"Dad, what is it?" Maia's mother asked. "What do you want?"

"Send... Maia... to Greece," he whispered.

A week later, Maia boarded an airplane to Athens.

CHAPTER 6

A FOOLISH GRIN ON HIS FACE

MAIA CONTINUED TO NAVIGATE her way through the crowded Athens airport.

"Maia! Hey, Maia! I see some of my group. Do you see your uncle?"

"Duh," Maia mumbled. After all, she'd never met her uncle before and wasn't sure what he looked like. But not wanting to be rude, Maia offered a simple "No."

The final piece of the puzzle in terms of Maia's return to Greece, after her grandmother had sent money for her airfare, had fallen into place when Maia's mother learned that her co-worker's niece Adriana was going to Greece as part of a youth ambassadorship program. Adriana would be a high school senior in the fall, was top in her class, and, as Maia heard over and over again during the ten-hour flight, was agonizing over whether to apply to Harvard or Princeton, or both. Still, as grating as Maia found Adriana, having someone to accompany her on the flight, especially someone as responsible (and dull) as Adriana, had extinguished any lingering concerns her mother had about letting Maia go.

Maia looked at the group of teenagers to which Adriana was pointing. They all had the same odd, desperate-to-be-hip look that Adriana possessed. Maia wondered what the appeal was of wearing a wool-knit tassel cap in the middle of summer, but seeing how quickly Adriana was drawn to the boy wearing one, she decided not to waste time thinking about it.

"I'm going to keep looking around for my uncle," Maia said, though it was obvious that "responsible" Adriana had forgotten all about her.

As she followed the crowd to the baggage claim area, Maia scanned faces for anyone who could be her uncle. Her mother had drilled the plan into her head nearly to the point of exhaustion. As soon as she passed through customs, Maia was to follow the signs to the baggage claim where her uncle would be waiting for her. As she came around a corner, Maia heard a loud buzzing, as if the airport was suddenly filled with a swarm of angry bees. There in the midst of a crowd of people stood a man holding a sign that read, "Maia of America."

Maia slowly exhaled. This was the moment she'd been waiting for and, just as when she showed her mother the letter from her grandmother that began this journey, it both frightened and excited her. Maia approached the man with the sign.

"Excuse me, but are you—"

A loud roar went up from the crowd. The man wasn't alone. An older woman pushed her way through the mass of people and reached out and embraced Maia. The woman shook her joyfully. When the woman finally pulled back and spoke, she said through tears, "I am grandmother," her accent thick but beautiful. The crowd continued to cheer, and Maia too found herself overwhelmed. Her grandmother drew her into another embrace, and this time, Maia hugged back, tears streaming down both their faces.

* * *

THE JOURNEY FROM THE AIRPORT to her grandmother's house was a blur. Many of Maia's relatives had turned up at the airport, and a veritable procession of cars had made its way to Varkiza, her grandmother's seaside town, which, like Sea Cliff, attracted visitors from near and far. All that mattered to Maia was that Varkiza was where she'd been born and where evidently much of her family continued to live. A few of her relatives spoke English, but most no better than her grandmother. After several hours of food, hugs, and tears, Maia was somewhat relieved when it appeared that most of her newfound family members would be leaving.

Maia stared out the dining room window. It was still light out, and Maia thought she could smell the sea, which was a source of familiar comfort given the joyful chaos she'd experienced since her arrival. Tired as she was, Maia was tempted by the idea of taking a walk down to the water.

Maia's grandmother returned from bidding goodbye to one of Maia's aunts. Or, Maia reconsidered, it really could've been someone she wasn't related to at all. It was as though the entire town had turned out to welcome Maia to Greece. Her grandmother took her by the hand.

"Come," she said, leading Maia down a long hallway. Her grandmother opened a door to a small bedroom. Long, thick curtains covered the wall opposite the door, but the room was bright and inviting.

"You sleep?" asked Maia's grandmother.

"Yes," Maia answered. "I'm a little tired from the trip."

Her grandmother pressed Maia's hands in her own and smiled. "Grandmother... very happy," she said.

Maia smiled in return. "I'm happy too."

Maia's grandmother hugged her again before leaving the room and closing the door. As she sat on the edge of the bed, Maia covered her mouth to keep from squealing. She'd done it! Maia let herself fall backward onto the bed. The sheets were soft and smelled like fresh-cut flowers. Rolling onto her stomach, Maia noticed a picture frame on the nightstand next to the bed. She reached over and picked it up. There were two people in the picture – a man and a woman – standing in front of the ruins of a temple on a hilltop. The woman was wearing a white dress and holding a bouquet of flowers. She was beautiful... and very familiar. And then it hit her – the picture was of Maia's parents on their wedding day.

Her mother looked the same, though there was a gleam in her eyes that Maia didn't recognize. The man standing beside her was smiling broadly, almost mugging for the camera. It was the first time she'd seen her father. In the days leading up to her trip, Maia learned that her mother hadn't kept any pictures of him. Her father had brown, curly hair and light eyes that appeared to dance even in the stillness of the picture. Maia scrutinized the wedding picture. Her mother and father both looked blissful, which made it even more difficult to understand why he would leave.

Maia placed the frame back on the nightstand. Looking around the room, she noticed more picture frames on top of the dresser. All of the pictures were of Maia as a baby, either with her parents or grandmother. It seemed so odd. They looked like the perfect family.

Maia stood and walked over to the curtains. Pulling them open, she was surprised to find that rather than a window, they covered a pair of glass doors leading to a small patio. Maia peered outside. The beach couldn't be too far. As she looked through the glass, a face popped up in front of her, causing Maia to jump. A boy about Maia's age stood on the other side of the doors, a foolish grin on his face. He was taller than Maia and, like her father, had a mop of curly, brown hair and pale blue eyes. Maia might have found him cute if he hadn't just scared her senseless, and if boys in general weren't basically annoying.

The boy started to speak, but Maia couldn't make out his words through the glass.

"I can't understand you," she said. The boy pointed to the handle and pantomimed turning it. Maia debated whether or not to open the door. The last thing she wanted at that moment was to muddle through yet another awkward conversation with yet another long lost relative, but the boy continued to grin and point enthusiastically at the handle. It appeared that Maia wouldn't get rid of him until he had his say.

Maia relented and turned the handle. She felt a rush of warm, salty air as she opened the door. Stepping down onto the patio, Maia could hear the cry of seagulls in the distance. It all reminded her so much of home. Meanwhile, the boy continued to grin at her.

"Um, hi," she offered with a weary smile, "I'm Maia."

"Yes, I know! It is wonderful to meet you!" responded the boy. He grabbed her by the hand and shook it vigorously.

Surprised by his command of English, Maia asked, "So, who are you?"

"Oh... I am your... cousin. I am Talos."

Maia rolled her eyes at the thought of having to remember another cousin's name. Still, she was relieved that this particular cousin spoke English well. Maia realized that Talos was still shaking her hand, and it was with some effort that she managed to pull herself free.

"Why weren't you here before?" Maia asked, not recognizing Talos as one of the many relatives that had descended upon her at the airport or on her grandmother's doorstep when she arrived.

"I had to travel farther than some of the others to get here."

"So, yeah… you, uh, speak English," Maia stated, unsure of where to take the conversation.

"Yes," replied Talos. "Do you speak Greek?"

"No, I didn't even know I was Greek until a few weeks ago. I'm still learning a lot of stuff. I can barely say 'hello' in Greek or remember half of the names of the gods."

"Well, that should not be of concern. There are some you are unlikely to meet." As soon as the words left his mouth, it was obvious that Talos regretted saying them. "Yes, well, never mind that," he said with a nervous laugh.

Maia scrunched up her face. With as many relatives as she was meeting, it would only make sense that one or two would be somewhat unbalanced. Glancing down at her feet, Maia noticed generous amounts of sand on the patio. She looked up at Talos, only to be aggravated by another foolish grin.

"How far is the beach?" Maia asked, turning in the direction of the sound of the seagulls.

"Oh, not far. Would you like me to show you?"

Maia looked back at the house. She didn't like the idea of slipping away without telling her grandmother, especially having just arrived.

Talos seemed to know what she was thinking. "We will not be gone long. Your grandmother will not notice."

Maia pulled the glass door closed. She hoped she wasn't making a mistake.

"Okay," she said, "but you have to promise me something."

"Of course!" replied Talos. "I will do anything you want!"

"You have to stop smiling at me like that. You're giving me the creeps."

CHAPTER 7

A SMALL BOW AND ARROW

AS PROMISED, the beach wasn't far away at all. As she neared it, Maia couldn't deny her attachment to the sea. It was, she realized, a constant in her life, and she smiled thinking about how something so simple could make her feel so at home. Though she was in a foreign place, Maia was surprised by how comforting she found the sights, sounds, and smells of her grandmother's town, especially when a breeze came up from the water.

Perhaps, Maia thought, she should start to think of it as her town as well. After all, she'd been born there, and if things had been different she might still live there. Somewhere in Varkiza, Maia was certain she'd find a place to sit and try to make sense of all of these thoughts. A bench by the water would do nicely, but she was open to suggestions.

Alongside her, Talos stumbled and Maia was reminded that she wasn't alone. As they walked, Maia observed that Talos was trying his best not to look directly at her – and failing miserably. It was becoming off-putting, and Maia kept a few feet away in case she felt the need to bolt. After coming all the way to Greece, she was having second thoughts about immediately putting her trust in a stranger merely because he spoke English. Maia thought about her lacrosse coach, Mrs. Finley, and how disappointed in Maia she'd be.

"When you're on the field, girls," Mrs. Finley would often start, "you can't let your guard down for a second." Maia and her teammates could count on Mrs. Finley to launch into her "be ever watchful" pep talk at least once per practice, drawing comparisons between the game of lacrosse and some of the more tragic historic examples of death and destruction caused by human error. "If you take your eyes off the ball for more than a heartbeat, you'll end up with another Titanic on your hands." Maia usually had to run extra laps around the track for rolling her eyes during these speeches, but as she watched Talos with a side-glance, she realized there was something to be respected about Mrs. Finley's philosophy.

"So, where did you learn English? Do they teach it in school?" Maia asked as casually as possible.

"Oh, no," Talos answered, "I do not go to school. I learn everything I need to know from my father, including English. He is one of the smartest men in all of Greece."

"Wow," said Maia, struggling to sound believable, "that's... great."

"Yes, I am sure he would have liked to have come to greet you himself, but he is very busy."

"It's okay. I've met more people today than I thought was possible."

"Your return has long been anticipated," said Talos excitedly.

"Yeah, well, I think I'm going to need a chart to try to remember who's who. While we're on the subject, Talos, how are we related?"

"Oh... your family and mine go back a long time... further than most, I imagine."

"What is that supposed to mean? Are we related or not?"

"In a manner of speaking, are we not all relatives?"

Before he could catch himself, Talos punctuated his question with a grin. He immediately looked down at his feet, hopeful that Maia hadn't noticed.

Maia was now fairly certain that the boy had something seriously wrong with him. Still, she decided to chalk up her uneasiness to jetlag and her own prejudices about the lack of intelligence of boys.

"Is it much farther?"

"We will be there very soon. Can you not hear the sound of the waves grow louder?"

Maia nodded. They walked in silence for another minute before arriving at the beach. It was peppered with white-and-blue-striped umbrellas, most of which were folded up since many of the day's beachgoers had left as the afternoon crawled into evening. Following a simple boardwalk made of thin, wooden planks from the road past a variety of stands, they stopped in a secluded spot a few yards away from the crystal-clear, blue water. Maia reached down and picked up a handful of sand, letting the fine grains slip between her fingers. She removed her shoes and socks and sat down near the remains of a large sandcastle. Talos took a seat beside her. Maia stared out at the sea. Inhaling deeply, she found herself at odds.

It was difficult not to think about her parents and wonder how much time they'd spent playing with her on this same beach. Growing up, Maia tried not to give more than a passing thought to her father. Since her mother never discussed him, Maia followed her lead. But now, in the place where she once had a father, Maia allowed herself to feel his loss.

Imagining that she was a child building castles in the sand, watched over by her parents, she took some comfort in knowing that her father must have loved her, even if his love wasn't enough to keep him from leaving her and her mother. Maia felt a swell of weariness wash over her. She closed her eyes, deciding it was best to leave these conflicting feelings to another time.

"It is beautiful, yes?" asked Talos.

Maia was glad for the distraction. Smiling, she opened her eyes.

"Yes," Maia answered. "It's very beautiful."

"You are happy you have come?" Talos asked.

"Very happy."

"Would you like to see... more?"

"I guess. Is there a lot more for you to show me?"

"Oh," said Talos, "there is much, much more." He got to his feet and walked in the direction of the boardwalk that led to the road. Talos stopped a few yards away from Maia and turned back to face her.

"Prepare to be amazed, Maia."

Maia looked over at him with a mix of curiosity and annoyance. What was it with this boy? Maia put on her socks and shoes and stood to face Talos.

"Alright," Maia began, "what's so amazing that... "

It took her a moment to realize that Talos was holding something in his hands. One terrifying second later, Maia recognized that what he was holding was a small bow and arrow. As Talos aimed the bow directly at her and released the arrow, Maia had the oddest thought.

My mother is never going to let me out of her sight again.

CHAPTER 8

A HORSE WITH WINGS

"MAIA."

Someone was saying her name, but it was muffled by the sound of waves breaking on sand.

"Maia, wake up."

Maia put her hand to her throbbing head and winced. When she opened her eyes and saw Talos standing over her with a silly grin, the understanding of what had just happened came flooding back.

"Hello," said Talos. "There, that was not so bad."

Maia jumped to her feet, lunging at Talos at the same time. He was sent sprawling onto his back. Maia searched the beach for the boardwalk back to the road, but nothing in her surroundings looked familiar.

Talos struggled to stand up, and Maia thought Mrs. Finley would've been proud of her for having completely knocked the wind out of him.

"Maia, please wait!" Talos called.

"Wait? Wait for what? For you to shoot another arrow at me?" Maia yelled, as she sprinted up the beach. The sand crept in between her toes, and Maia realized that she wasn't wearing her own clothes. Instead of her jeans, hooded sweatshirt, and sneakers, Maia was clothed in a cranberry-colored tunic and leather sandals. Looking over her shoulder, Maia saw that Talos was wearing a similar outfit in white. Had he changed their clothes when she was unconscious?

"What a freak!" Maia spat.

"Maia, I will not chase you. Please, you must let me explain."

When she had about thirty yards of distance between her and Talos, Maia stopped and again tried to orient herself. The beach was empty. Not only was the boardwalk gone, but the umbrellas and stands were missing too. In the distance, the water was speckled with small, wooden fishing boats. Looking up and down the shoreline, Maia searched for signs of the houses, shops, or other landmarks she and Talos had passed on their way to the beach, but everything familiar was gone.

Talos called out to her, his face pale. "Please, I can explain. If you come back, I will explain everything."

Maia glared at him. At least he'd finally stopped grinning. "Why did you shoot that arrow at me?" she snapped.

"I was not trying to hurt you. See, you have no injuries."

It was true. Though her head still throbbed, she didn't appear to be injured.

"It was the only way I could bring you here," Talos said.

"Where are we?"

"This is my home, Maia. And in some ways, it is your home as well."

Maia scowled. "Explain."

"I will. I promise. Just follow me up the beach and I will take you to my father."

Maia weighed what few options she had. "Why should I trust you?"

Talos grinned, which Maia found both infuriating and tempting – he hardly needed to give her a reason to knock the stupid smile off his face. Talos walked toward her, and Maia looked him over carefully as he approached. Despite his height, she was confident that she could take him down.

"So, start explaining," Maia said.

Talos opened his mouth but before he could speak, a rather large, white bird – or so Maia thought initially – flew over their heads and landed some twenty feet away. Startled as she was, it was several seconds before Maia realized that it wasn't a bird but a horse with wings. Her mouth agape, she watched as the animal flapped its powerful wings while sniffing through a large patch of beach grass.

"Oh, my god," whispered Maia. "How is that... how is that possible?"

"I know," said Talos. "It must have broken away from the herd. My father is not going to be happy."

Maia stared at the fantastic-looking animal before her. She'd never seen anything so beautiful. Maia remembered reading about a winged horse during one of her many trips to the library but struggled to recall its name.

"There's a herd of them?" she asked.

"Oh, yes," answered Talos. "There used to be just one, but now there are many. My father helps to make sure they are protected and for the most part well contained."

"I don't understand," said Maia, shaking her head. "Where are we?" she asked as she continued to stare at the horse.

"You may think of it as having 'turned a corner'," Talos answered, a smile lighting up his face.

Unable to suppress her curiosity, Maia approached the horse as it nuzzled around in the beach grass. Its wings were larger than any Maia had ever seen on an animal, and its long, ivory mane shimmered in the sunlight. Maia found herself lifting her hand to reach out and stroke it.

"I think that one is called Pierinos," said Talos. The horse raised its head, aware that it wasn't alone. "Yes, he has a brown, crescent-shaped mark on his nose."

Maia stretched out her hand. Before she could get close enough to touch the animal, the horse reared back and, giving a loud, high-pitched cry, spread its massive wings and took to the sky over the water.

Talos said, "Father is working on a way of catching them when they break away from the herd, but it is not yet perfected."

"You're not amazed by that?"

"By what?"

"Pierinos. You're used to seeing horses with wings?"

"I am used to seeing much more than that," Talos replied.

Maia watched the horse shrink in the distance. Her whole body quivered. Maia turned and looked to the distant hills that surrounded the beach. "We're not in Greece anymore, are we?" she asked.

"In a way we are. Will you allow me to explain?"

Maia nodded, even though she doubted that any explanation Talos offered would soothe the fear underlying her curiosity.

CHAPTER 9

THE TRUTH ABOUT HER FATHER

"LIKE MANY STORIES in the history of Greece, this one involves a war. Some have called it the Great War. It almost destroyed everything the gods had spent centuries building."

"What gods are you talking about? The Greek gods?"

"As if there are any others," answered Talos. "Yes, I speak of the gods of Olympus."

"But Talos, they're not real. They're about as real as—"

"Winged horses?"

Maia relented. "Okay, I get it. Go on."

Talos continued. "At the end of the Great War, Lord Zeus, father and king of gods and man, looked over all of the destruction that had been caused and placed the blame on the gods themselves for interfering too often in the affairs of man. He feared their followers would lose faith and, without the people's faith in them, the gods would face extinction." Talos turned and looked directly at Maia. "Lord Zeus would not allow their extinction to come to pass."

"And so," Talos said, waving his arms in a grand gesture, "the gods created this world, a perfect replica of Greece as it existed before the Great War. All of the most extraordinary aspects of what you would call 'ancient' Greece were brought here. Every fantastic creature, the most loyal of followers, and the gods themselves left your world and settled here, where it was as if the Great War had never happened. The people never had reason to lose their faith in the gods, thereby assuring their continued existence."

Talos stopped speaking and again locked eyes with Maia. "Wondrous, is it not?"

"Yeah, it's wondrous, alright. Except that I don't believe a word of it," Maia told him. "I don't know what your deal is, but the gods of Olympus only exist in stories. I should know. I spent hours reading books of Greek mythology in the library." Maia paused. "I don't know where we are, but I want to go back to my grandmother's house."

"Hmmm," said Talos, scratching his head. "I really thought the winged horse might have made this go easier."

Maia almost smiled but caught herself. "Talos, even if I wanted to believe you, what you're telling me just doesn't make sense. How could there be a place where the gods are actually real? Am I supposed to think that any second now, a god in a chariot is going to soar through the sky and make the sun set?"

"No, of course not," said Talos, smirking. "The sun will not set for a few hours."

Maia glared. "Talos—"

"Wait. Let me explain further. The gods were real. I mean, they are real. But when they created this world, they completely left yours. That is why you believe they exist only in myths. This world is not so different from yours except in one significant respect. The people here never had reason to stop believing in the gods. And because of that, in this world, what you dismiss as myths are very much real."

Talos punctuated his tale with a broad grin, which, to Maia's surprise, was becoming a little less aggravating.

"That arrow must've hit me harder than I thought because I was starting to think you were telling the truth for a second."

"Come with me," said Talos. "There is so much I want to show you."

Maia looked out at the water and thought about her mother. She too had been drawn in by a mysterious Greek with a flashy smile. Things hadn't turned out too well for her mother, but Maia decided to push that out of her head for the moment.

"Okay, but first you have to explain how I got into this outfit."

Talos laughed. "One of my father's inventions. Our clothing changed when we crossed over. What we are wearing is common to most people here."

"So, you didn't—"

"No, of course not!" Talos blurted out.

Maia breathed easily. She could at least put that worry to rest.

"It is a necessary change," Talos said, collecting himself. "It would not do for you to be seen in your regular clothes. The people here have never seen someone from your world, nor would they accept that such a place exists."

"So, who does know?"

"Only a chosen few," said Talos with pride, "like me and my—"

"Father, right, I get it," interrupted Maia. She was beginning to think Talos had more of an issue with his father than she did with hers.

"Yes, my father and a few trusted others," Talos continued. "But for the most part, the gods do not want the people to know."

"Why not? Are they afraid people might want to leave?" Maia asked.

Talos gave Maia a very serious look. Catching himself, he quickly said, "Why would anyone want to leave here? Can you think of a more wondrous place? You will see, Maia. You will love it here so much that you will never want to leave."

Maia didn't care for the way that sounded, but she decided to take Talos's assertion as mere excitement and to ignore the troubling undertone for the moment. "Why don't you just show me around some more," Maia suggested.

"The village is not far," Talos said. "In fact, this will give us a chance to—"

Talos was interrupted by a loud, lingering squeal, as a young woman dressed in a scanty, white robe burst onto the beach, running for the water. Maia barely had time to take in the spectacle of the woman when a dark, squat man with large, pointy ears and long, curly hair leapt onto the sand in pursuit. Maia blushed as she caught a few words from the man about what he intended to do to the woman if he caught her.

Peals of laughter came from the woman as she reached the surf. Before the man could get within a few feet of her, the woman dove beneath the waves, surfacing several yards out. She waved playfully at the hairy, little man who stood at the water's edge, cursing and stomping his feet. When the woman disappeared under the water again, the man turned around and saw that he was being watched. Grumbling, he scratched his bottom before breaking into a run and diving behind a large clump of beach grass.

"Satyrs never learn. With those short legs, they will never catch one."

"Catch what?" Maia asked, still shaken from the failed assault she'd just witnessed.

"A nymph," Talos answered, a distinct gleam in his eyes. "But then, who could blame the satyrs for trying?"

* * *

AS THEY WALKED toward the village, Talos pointed out various landmarks, including the place he said Maia's grandmother's house stood back in her world.

"So, the land and water and everything else are physically the same?" Maia asked curiously.

"Yes. When the gods created this place, they captured everything that existed in your world at that moment and brought it here. In fact, while the temples and other tributes to the gods in your world crumbled, here they stand proudly still. Those people that stayed behind hardly noticed when the glory of the gods left because so many of them had already ceased to have faith. With the gods gone, it was not long before the rest of your world stopped believing as well."

"But what about here? The same thing could happen. Aren't the gods worried that the people here could lose faith?"

Talos appeared not to have heard Maia's question. Instead, his attention was drawn in the direction of the water.

"Can you hear that?" he asked Maia, practically bouncing up and down.

Maia could make out the faint sound of singing. "What is it?" she asked.

Talos was enraptured – a sheepish grin all but masked his face. "A siren!" he finally exclaimed. "She must be trying to lure the fishermen as they return to port. Let us see what happens!"

Though she was an excellent runner, Maia found herself struggling to keep up with Talos. As they ran through the village and got closer to the port, the singing became louder. Maia could see that Talos wasn't alone in his excitement. It appeared as though most of the men in the village had rushed to hear the siren's intoxicating call. Maia looked to where many in the crowd were pointing. There in the harbor, on an outcrop of rocks, lay the source of the singing.

The siren had long green hair and a tail greener still. Unlike the mermaids Maia was used to seeing in cartoons or on the shelves of toy stores, she wasn't wearing a flower in her hair and her chest wasn't covered with a clamshell bra. This siren was less refined and more mischievous in appearance. Maia watched the men around her, all looking as ridiculous as Talos and all oblivious to the fishing boats that were drawing perilously close to the rocks.

"Is she not beautiful?" Talos asked.

"But don't you see what's about to happen? The men in those boats will be killed."

"It would be worth dying to spend eternity under the waves with her," said a crooked, old man with a cane standing beside Maia. Craning his neck to get a better view, the old man nearly fell on top of Talos. Maia looked from young fool to old with annoyance.

Suddenly, the siren's song was blocked out by what sounded like the loud blast of a trumpet. As the siren dove from the rocks into the water, Talos and the other men around Maia gradually began to regain their senses. Maia looked around for the source of the blast.

"Triton had to ruin it," said Talos.

"Who are you talking about?" asked Maia.

"The sea god," said Talos, pointing past the outcrop of rocks. "Out there."

In the middle of the harbor, rising up from the water, was a large man with a long, white beard that glistened in the sun. He held a large conch shell. Awestruck, Maia watched as the sea god raised the shell to his lips and sounded another loud blast. The fishing boats that were lingering close to the rocks were instantly blown to safety. On the shore, the crowd cheered as the sea god disappeared beneath the surface of the water.

"You see, Maia," said Talos, at last recovered from the siren's mesmerizing song, "that is why the people will not lose their faith. The gods protect us."

"This is going to sound strange, but I think I've seen him before," Maia said. "In my town. Yes! Triton was in the harbor in my town!"

The crowd began to disperse, leaving only a few people other than Maia and Talos at the port.

"Why would a sea god be in my world? In my town?" Maia asked.

Talos stared off in the distance, ignoring her questions. "Come," he said, "I have more to show you."

"No! I'm not going anywhere else with you! I've put up with a lot today, the least of which was being shot with an arrow. You said no one here leaves, so why would Triton be in my town?"

Talos looked down at his feet. "Some leave," he mumbled.

"Like who, Talos? The gods? Your father?" asked Maia. "You were obviously able to leave."

Talos continued staring downward. "I should not be the one to tell you this."

"Tell me what, Talos?" Maia demanded, no longer awed by the wonder of all she'd seen. But Talos kept silent.

"Why did you bring me here?" Maia asked. "You need to tell me."

"I thought you should see it," Talos answered, still avoiding eye contact. "I thought you should see the place that meant so much to your father."

"My father? What does my father have to do with anything?" asked Maia, making little effort to control her growing anger.

"Your father has to do with everything here! If not for his sacrifice, this world would have ceased to exist!" Talos said, finally looking Maia in the eyes.

The shock on Maia's face signaled Talos to stop speaking.

"I... I should not say anymore. Please, let me bring you to my father. He can explain."

Maia grabbed Talos by the front of his tunic and shook him. "What sacrifice, Talos? Tell me what you're talking about – now!"

Talos's voice trembled. "Maia, this is where your family is from. They were allowed to leave, but not without promising that when the time came, your father would return. That is why, just after you were born, your father had to leave you. He sacrificed everything to preserve this world."

Maia struggled to take in what she was hearing. Had Talos said that her father died when she was just a baby? The meaning of his words swept over Maia in waves. There would be no reunion with her father. There would be no joyous phone call to her mother. Standing by the sea in a strange place inhabited by mermaids, nymphs, and winged horses, Maia allowed herself to admit the hope she'd buried deep inside. She'd come to Greece to find her father in the chance that she could make things right between her parents – that her family would be complete again.

Maia felt Talos's eyes on her, but wouldn't give him the gratification of looking back. She took a deep breath. "Take me home, Talos."

"Maia, please let me—"

"No, you've said enough!" Maia interrupted. "I'm done. You brought me here against my will, and you tell me my father is gone and... "

Maia stopped. A profound sadness was welling up inside her, but she didn't want to cry – not in this place; not in front of Talos.

She thought of her mother and how she'd spent Maia's entire life trying to protect her from this pain. What would her mother say now? Pushing this question out of her mind, Maia started walking back to the beach.

"Where are you going?" Talos called after her.

Maia didn't know how she would get home, but she couldn't bear staying in the place where the hope of reuniting with her father had been dashed. The people of what was in another reality her grandmother's seaside village paid her little attention as she walked its sandy streets. Talos followed a few paces behind, but he was perceptive enough to stop trying to engage Maia. As she approached the beach, Maia looked skyward. The sun would be setting soon, and she wondered whether a god in a chariot would indeed be streaking across the sky.

Maia turned around to face Talos. The boy stood in place and shifted his feet, visibly troubled by how their excursion had unraveled.

"How do I get home?" Maia asked.

"I have to bring you to my father. He can send you back."

Maia gritted her teeth. Talos was going to get what he wanted after all.

"Where is he?"

"Not far. We can—"

Talos was interrupted by the sound of a wagon being pulled by a team of horses as it rushed down the road in their direction. An older man dressed in clothing similar to Talos's held the reins. The horses came to a stop, and Talos called out to the driver.

"Father! We were just coming to see you! This is—"

"I know."

Climbing down from the wagon, Talos's father walked toward them. Unlike his son, he showed little tendency toward smiling.

Maia, pleased by the arrival of the man she'd been promised could send her home, ignored the tension between Talos and his father and spoke more forcefully than she thought she could manage in light of everything she'd experienced today.

"I want to be sent home!"

"And home you will go," Talos's father replied, as he continued to look with disapproval at his son.

"How did... how did you find us, Father?"

"Her presence was noticed." Talos's father turned to Maia. "It is time for you to go."

"Fine by me," Maia answered.

Talos's father held out his hand to help Maia onto the wagon. Maia complied and took a seat next to Talos, who'd already scrambled aboard.

Taking the reins, Talos's father commanded the horses to be off. "I take it my son has explained to you certain things about this world?"

Maia nodded.

"What he may not have explained is that it is not wise for you to be here. I would not suggest you return."

Maia resisted the urge to tell Talos's father that he was as deluded as his son, but didn't think it was best to antagonize the man who promised to send her home. Regardless of his warning, she had no intention of returning to this place.

After a few minutes, the wagon came to a stop at the location Maia recognized as where Talos had said her grandmother's house would be back in her world. Talos's father climbed down and helped Maia off the wagon. Talos jumped off and stood next to his father, his head bowed.

"I am sorry for this," Talos's father said.

"It's not your—" Maia started to say, only to be met with a flash of blinding, white light. Stumbling backward, Maia fell to the ground. As her sight returned, Maia was relieved to see that she was on her grandmother's patio. Glancing around to make sure she hadn't been seen, she entered her bedroom through the sliding glass doors. Her clothing had returned to normal and her watch showed that she'd been away for a little less than two hours.

Maia sat on the edge of the bed, her mind a turbulent sea of words and images. She looked at the picture of her parents on their wedding day. Her hand trembling, Maia slammed the frame facedown on the nightstand. After what she'd been told, there was little point in being reminded of how happy her parents had once been.

Maia didn't move for several minutes. She tried not to cry, but when the tears came, she couldn't stop them. Alone, in a land far more foreign than she could have dreamed, Maia longed for her mother's arms to hold and comfort her. But more than that, she longed for something else – that she'd never sought out the truth about her father.

CHAPTER 10

MANY WONDROUS THINGS

THE NEXT FEW DAYS passed uneventfully. No one appeared to notice Maia's absence on the day of her arrival or her sullen mood since. Her grandmother was still overjoyed by Maia's presence. Countless relatives and family friends had shown up daily at the house to visit, making it difficult for Maia to stay in her room as she was inclined to do after her experience in the "other" Greece. Maia also had several cousins her age who were eager to bring her to the beach or to hang out in the town square. As much as she tried to put out of her mind what Talos had told her about her family's origins, Maia often found herself examining her grandmother and the others for some sign. In the end, she decided it was best to say as little as possible to anyone until she knew whom she could trust.

Maia spoke to her mother before going to bed on the day she'd arrived in Greece. At first she wanted to tell her what had happened, but Maia was afraid her mother wouldn't believe her or worse yet insist that she come home. As troubled as she'd been by her unexpected trip with Talos, Maia wasn't ready to leave, at least not until she had more of her questions answered, however painful that might prove. She owed as much to her mother.

One morning after breakfast, Maia's grandmother told her that she had a surprise. Maia braced herself in case her grandmother pulled out a bow and arrow. Instead, in her rudimentary English, she told Maia that they were going to Athens to tour the Acropolis.

Maia nearly jumped out of her seat. Since she'd first thought about traveling to Greece, there were few things Maia was looking forward to as much as visiting the archeological remains in Athens. It was "where the gods once walked," she remembered reading in reference to the Acropolis. Since her experience with Talos, this notion had taken on even greater meaning.

Maia's grandmother explained that they would be going with her uncle Dorian – the only unmarried one – and her cousin Helena, who similar to Maia had just turned thirteen. Maia liked Helena, and on one of their trips to the beach together she'd been tempted to ask Helena if she knew about the world Talos had shown her. However, within moments of meeting her, Maia learned that Helena had only two interests – looking at boys and talking about boys. Still, Maia was glad Helena was coming to Athens, especially since she spoke English very well. There was something else about Helena that Maia liked. She reminded Maia not to take everything so seriously.

Maia realized that her grandmother was staring at her. This had happened several times in the past few days. Maia often let her mind wander when her grandmother attempted to speak to her. She wanted to pay attention, but it was difficult to understand her. And Maia was also distracted by the idea that her grandmother was keeping a secret from her. Still, she looked innocent enough, and Maia wanted to like her, especially when her grandmother smiled at her and Maia supposed she recognized her own smile on her grandmother's face.

A short while later, as her grandmother cleaned up in the kitchen after refusing Maia's help, her uncle Dorian arrived. Maia liked Uncle Dorian too. He wasn't loud and overbearing like her other uncles, and even Helena, who had little patience for anyone over the age of eighteen, thought he was alright. The more time

Maia spent with Uncle Dorian, the more she hoped that his personality was similar to her father's and that, perhaps if the time was right, she might ask him about the "other" Greece.

After he spoke with her grandmother in the kitchen, Uncle Dorian joined Maia on the patio where she was reading her Greek travel book.

"Good morning, Maia. Did your grandmother tell you where we are going?" Uncle Dorian asked.

"She did," Maia replied. "Helena is coming too?"

"Yes. Her father will drop her off soon. Today is a good day to go. It can be very hot on the Acropolis, but today it will be pleasant enough to enjoy all that the site has to offer."

Uncle Dorian took a seat next to Maia at the patio table and glanced at her book. "You are reading about the Parthenon?"

"Yes," answered Maia. Sensing an opportunity to probe for information, she added, "It says here that the Parthenon was built on the Acropolis thousands of years ago to honor the goddess Athena. I can't imagine that."

"Faith is a powerful force," said Uncle Dorian. "Judged alone on the beliefs that led to its creation, the Acropolis is truly a wondrous place."

Maia perked up at her uncle's use of the same word Talos used to describe his world.

"What sort of things do you find wondrous, Uncle Dorian?" Maia asked.

"Wondrous?" her uncle repeated. "Well, you can find many wondrous things if you know where to look."

"Is the Acropolis a good place to look?"

"Perhaps," said Uncle Dorian with a wink. "You will have to let me know what, if anything, you find wondrous."

Maia nodded her head, but quickly looked down and frowned. Uncle Dorian's comment was innocent enough, but it still further fueled her overall lack of trust.

Uncle Dorian continued speaking. "So, you have been meeting many family members?"

"Yes." Maia couldn't help but laugh as she answered. "Many! I'd no idea."

"We are all very happy that you have come. For years we have wanted your mother to bring you."

Maia sensed another opportunity to find out what her uncle knew. "I don't think she has many good memories of this place."

Uncle Dorian grimaced. "It pains me to hear that, Maia. Your mother and I were quite close, and she was very happy here. But after your father... "

Uncle Dorian's voice trailed off as he gazed skyward. Maia watched him for a few moments before speaking.

"Uncle Dorian, what do you think happened to my father?"

Her uncle looked Maia directly in the eyes, and he was about to speak when a commotion broke out in the house. Uncle Dorian stood and hurried inside with Maia following. She could hear several raised voices. Helena came rushing up to Maia and grabbed her by the hand, pulling her back onto the patio.

"Helena, what's going on?"

"Oh, it is nothing. My father is all upset over something with a boy. Do not worry. Yaya and Uncle Dorian will calm him."

Maia looked her cousin over. She was wearing cut-off jeans and a very tight shirt. Helena was a few inches taller than Maia, and she'd already developed in ways that would attract the immediate attention of most teenage boys. Helena was looking at herself too, or at least at her reflection in the glass patio doors that led into the kitchen.

"Do you like this shirt?" she asked Maia. "I can get you one."

"It's nice," Maia replied, though she doubted it would look as good on her as it did on Helena.

"I want to look stylish when I go to the city. I hardly ever get to go," Helena said, as she adjusted and readjusted her hair. "It can be so boring in this town."

"I don't think it's so bad," Maia said.

"That is because it is new to you. Soon, you too will be bored."

Given her experiences so far, Maia doubted that, but she nodded anyway.

Inside the house, the yelling continued, though Helena appeared to take little notice.

"Does your father always yell like that?" Maia asked.

"Yes," answered Helena, "especially when it comes to boys." Helena took Maia's hand again. "That reminds me. Let me tell you about the boy I saw at the port this morning."

It took tremendous willpower for Maia not to roll her eyes.

CHAPTER 11

A PLACE LIKE THIS

UNCLE DORIAN WAS RIGHT – it was a beautiful day to visit the Acropolis. Maia was eager to see the site, but they had to wait on a long line to enter. Helena chattered nonstop the whole time, until her grandmother yelled at her to take a break. Maia's grandmother had some difficulty with the many steps leading up to the entrance, but with Uncle Dorian's occasional assistance she was able to manage them. She smiled at Maia as they neared the gates. Whatever had happened back in the house with Helena's father had been forgotten.

Maia's heart raced as she crossed through the entrance to the Acropolis. There before her was the Parthenon, more beautiful than in any photograph she'd seen. Even partially covered with scaffolding, the temple dedicated to the goddess Athena was a stunning sight.

Uncle Dorian leaned into Maia and asked, "Do you sense anything wondrous yet?"

Maia smiled politely at her uncle. Was he mocking her?

"Not yet, Uncle Dorian. I'll let you know."

Her uncle smiled back at Maia. "Let me then point out some of the many landmarks on the Acropolis." As Uncle Dorian spoke, Maia listened to every word but couldn't wait to venture on her own.

"The Acropolis has survived centuries of war and destruction. We are very fortunate to be able to stand here today," said Uncle

Dorian. "The Parthenon is of course the central structure to this ancient fortress, but there are several others of great importance and beauty, such as the Temple of Athena Nike, that we will visit."

Uncle Dorian turned his attention back to Maia. "Perhaps you and Helena would like to explore the Parthenon while I wait in the shade with your grandmother for her to rest a bit."

Helena let out a shriek and, for at least the tenth time that day, grabbed Maia by the hand and pulled her away. While Helena rattled on, Maia looked around in awe. After dreaming about visiting the Acropolis for the last several weeks, she was actually there. The intensity of the moment was almost enough to make her forget about her misadventure with Talos.

After a few minutes of unexpected silence, Maia realized that Helena was no longer beside her. Maia spotted her a few yards back talking to a teenage boy handing out pamphlets. Maia couldn't hear what was being said, but Helena kept tossing her head back and laughing.

"Unbelievable," Maia muttered. With everything there was to see at the Acropolis, Helena still had eyes only for boys. A young woman approached Maia and handed her a pamphlet. Looking away from her cousin, who was still squealing with laughter at everything the boy said, Maia turned her attention to the pamphlet the woman had given her.

"Return the Parthenon sculptures to Greece," Maia read. She looked up at the temple. Had something been taken from here? She walked around the corner to get a better look at the pediment. As she stopped to read some more, Maia realized that someone was coming toward her. She lifted her head to explain that she already had a pamphlet, but as she started to speak Maia was blinded by a flash of white light.

Before she could regain her sight, Maia tripped, landing on her knee. As she cried out in pain, a hand pulled her by the forearm to her feet.

"Quiet!" a gruff voice commanded. "Do not make another sound."

As her vision returned, Maia tried to make sense of what had happened. She stiffened as she realized that the bearded man in front of her was wearing a tunic. Maia turned from side to side. Other people around her were also wearing tunics and robes. She looked down and cringed to see that she was wearing similar clothing. Maia was back in the other world.

Towering in front of her, the Parthenon appeared as if it had been built that very day. The scaffolding was gone and the pediment was filled with sculptures painted in a stunning array of colors. The columns holding up the pediment were a dazzling white. Maia would have continued to stare if the man hadn't grabbed her and pulled her away.

"Hey!" Maia yelled. "Let go of me!"

The bearded man reeled around and struck Maia across the face. "You will be silent!" he shouted.

Her face stinging from the blow, a wave of panic rushed through Maia's body. As unsettling as her trip to the other world with Talos had been, she hadn't experienced fear. As the man continued to pull at Maia, tears welled in her eyes. Where was the bearded man taking her? Maia thought about her mother and as her fear that she would never see her again grew so did her resolve to break free from the man's grip. Her mother hadn't raised her to be weak. Wiping her eyes, Maia steeled herself for a getaway.

As they broke through the crowd, Maia made herself trip, causing the bearded man to loosen his grip just enough that she was able to break free. At the same time, she kicked the man hard in the ankle. As he fell to his knee growling in pain, Maia scrambled to her feet and sprinted off. The bearded man shouted for Maia to stop, but she darted her way through the crowd, heading in the direction of the Parthenon. Running up the steps, Maia's panic swelled as she realized that this time there was no one to help her return home. She needed Talos – goofy grin and all.

After she entered the temple, Maia came to a quick stop. The people in the Parthenon seemed indifferent to her presence. Certain the bearded man was in pursuit, Maia ran and hid behind a large statue of the goddess Athena in the center of the building.

Struggling to catch her breath, Maia was afraid she didn't have much time before the bearded man caught up with her. As she looked for a way to escape, Maia heard him call out to her. His voice echoed through the temple.

"Come out now!"

Maia sprinted in the opposite direction, exited the Parthenon, and collided with a young woman wearing bright red robes, sending them both sprawling to the ground.

"I'm sorry," Maia said, as she helped the woman get to her feet.

"You should be more careful!" the woman in red robes cried out. "This is not a place for children to be running."

"I know, but I need help. There's a man—" Maia began, but the woman walked away before she could finish.

Maia resisted the urge to follow the woman, and instead ducked beside the steps leading into the Parthenon. Beads of sweat dotted her forehead as her breath grew more and more shallow. It was difficult to think of what to do next.

"Oh, look at her!" said a shrill voice from above.

"What is she wearing?" asked another equally sharp voice.

Maia looked around but couldn't find the source of the voices.

"She should not be here."

"No, of course she should not be here. This is entirely the boy's fault."

"Stop!" Maia cried. "Please, where are you? A man is chasing me and—"

"No good can come of this. No good at all," interrupted a voice followed by a loud squawk.

Maia looked above her. Perched on the edge of the pediment were two crows. Were they staring at her? One of the crows turned its head in the direction of the other.

"I will tell you what else is no good. The color of her clothing is awful," the crow screeched.

Maia almost fell backwards. "You can talk!"

"Not too bright, is she?" asked the other crow.

"I'm sorry, it's just that I'm not used to, well, I'm not used to anything here. And that man... he's trying to take me. Can you tell me how to get out of here?"

The crows glared at her for several seconds. Finally, one turned to the other and said, "We really have no choice."

"Oh, fine. Follow us. We will lead you to safety."

The crows took flight and Maia bounded after them, racing through the crowds on the Acropolis. Everyone she passed appeared oblivious to her plight and Maia wondered what if anything the people of this world would find unusual. After several minutes, the crows landed on a large rock beside the Temple of Athena Nike. Nearly out of breath, Maia threw herself to the ground beside them.

"You can stay here only for a moment."

"What did the man chasing you look like?"

"He was wearing blue. And he had dark, curly hair and a beard and... " Maia realized she was describing many of the men she'd seen in the crowd.

The crows looked at each other and squawked. "You should not be here," one of them said.

"I know that!" Maia replied. "I didn't want to come here, this time or the first time!"

"You did not come here on your own?"

"No! Of course not! It was the man with the beard. I was with my family. There was a flash of light and... oh, why am I arguing with a couple of crows?" Maia said.

The birds continued as if Maia weren't there.

"Daedalus is not going to be happy."

Maia thought the name sounded familiar but, as with the winged horse, couldn't place it. Her mind was too clouded with worry – or was it something else?

"Oh, and the boy. He will surely be punished for having started this."

"The others are getting very bold. Bringing the girl here was very bold indeed."

"Who are you talking about? Why would anyone else want to bring me here?" Maia asked.

One of the crows flew onto Maia's shoulder and cocked its head, as it looked her in the eye.

"What you do not know is that a war has been brewing for centuries – a war in which you may play a very important role."

"Your existence may be the basis upon which the future of this world is decided," added the other crow.

"But why me?" Maia asked. "My father already sacrificed himself. Wasn't that enough?"

The crows didn't have the opportunity to answer. As the one sitting on the rock swiftly took flight, the crow on Maia's shoulder let out a loud squawk as it fell to the ground in front of her, a knife protruding from its breast. Maia gasped. The bearded man was standing a few feet away. He lumbered forward and spit as he pulled the short knife from the body of the crow. The bearded man brought the knife to Maia's throat.

"You will come with me now. And if you try to run, you will find yourself at rest forever in the Elysian Fields," said the bearded man.

He grabbed Maia by the wrist and pulled her to her feet. Maia allowed the bearded man to lead her past the gates and away from the Acropolis. When she gained the presence of mind to pull away, the bearded man turned on his heel and lifted her by her wrist onto the tips of her toes. Through short, hot breaths, he said, "It is better not to fight. You will only give me reason to hurt... "

The bearded man looked over her head and cursed. Maia looked to the sky as well. Someone was flying toward them on the back of a winged horse. As they got closer, Maia's face brightened as she recognized the horse as Pierinos and the rider upon his back as Talos. They swooped down as Talos gave a loud cry. He was carrying a spear that he threw with impressive accuracy at the bearded man, grazing his arm but missing Maia completely. With her captor distracted by Talos's attack, Maia was able to break free from his grip just before Talos and the winged horse swooped down again on the bearded man, knocking him to the ground. Talos landed Pierinos next to Maia and reached out his hand.

"Come with me, please. It is not safe here."

Maia thought that was pretty obvious, but she grabbed Talos's hand and allowed him to pull her onto Pierinos. Talos shouted to the horse and it reared back and took flight. Maia wrapped her arms around Talos's waist.

"How did you know I was here?"

"My father knew. He sent me. I think he wants me to prove myself trustworthy again."

"Who was that man?" Maia asked.

"He is unimportant," Talos assured her. "The only thing that matters is sending you home."

"Talos, what exactly have you gotten me involved in?"

"I made a mistake, Maia. It was a great error on my part to think I could bring you here and not have it noticed. But even my father did not think they would try to bring you here themselves."

"You're still not telling me what's really going on." Maia paused. "Talos, do I have something to do with a war?"

"Did that man speak to you of the war? Even I knew better than to bring it up."

"It wasn't the man. It was, um, a crow, actually," Maia said.

"A crow told you that? That is not possible."

"We're on the back of a winged horse, and you're going to argue with me about whether a crow can talk?"

Talos signaled for Pierinos to land next to the Parthenon, amidst a crowd of puzzled onlookers. He helped Maia off the horse's back.

"Here, take this." Talos handed Maia a silver bracelet. "Put it on and do not take it off. As long as you wear it, they will not be able to pull you back, even in a place like this."

"What does that mean?" asked Maia, as she slipped the bracelet onto her wrist.

"There are certain locations where the barrier between our two worlds is weaker. Usually, they are places where the gods were once heavily worshipped or others like your grandmother's town, which are important for other reasons."

Maia ignored Talos's last comment and studied the bracelet on her wrist. "If I wear this, I can't be brought back here?"

"No," Talos answered, "you will be safe. Now, please, shield your—"

"No, wait! The crow—"

"Maia, of course I believe that a crow spoke to you. I just do not understand why it would tell you about the war."

"No, I mean, it said a name – Daedalus. Who is that?" Maia asked.

"Lord Zeus!" Talos exclaimed. "It is a miracle that any secrets are kept with all of the crows we have squawking about our property. If you must know, Daedalus is my father. And as long as I am revealing things, you should know that my name is not really Talos."

"What? Why would you—"

Before Maia could finish her question, the boy she thought was named Talos pulled something from his belt, releasing a bright flash of light. Momentarily blinded, Maia nearly tripped again. As she regained her sight, she could see the Parthenon before her, but the temple again showed the wear of time. She was back in her own world. Maia looked around but no one seemed surprised by her sudden reappearance. She took a moment to collect her thoughts and then started walking back to where her uncle and grandmother were supposed to be resting.

"Maia, there you are! Where were you?"

Helena ran toward her. Maia tried to speak but found herself at a loss for words. What possible explanation could she offer?

"Uncle Dorian, I found her!" Helena called.

Uncle Dorian came running over. Maia's grandmother, who'd been speaking to a security officer, came trailing after.

"Maia, thank god! Where did you disappear to?" asked Uncle Dorian.

As she neared, Maia could see that her grandmother was crying.

"I was listening to a tour guide," Maia lied. "There was a group of American tourists, and I started listening to their guide talk about the Parthenon. I guess I lost track of time."

"What happened to your knee?" asked Helena, pointing to a dark bruise on Maia's left knee from when she'd tripped earlier.

"Oh, I fell walking back here. I stopped for a few minutes to rest." Maia was surprised by how easily the lies came.

Her grandmother's face reflected an uneasy mix of relief and concern. Maia wondered how long she'd been gone as well as how many lies she would need to tell before her grandmother would stop looking so pained.

"Well, Maia, please try not to do that again," Uncle Dorian said, poorly masking his distress. "Your grandmother thought your mother would curse the day she let you come to Greece."

Uncle Dorian put his hand on Maia's shoulder and gave her a sort of half-smile, the same her mother usually gave her when she wanted to reprimand Maia but was afraid of putting her in an adolescent snit. Maia saw that look on her mother's face quite often and was amazed to see how easily it transcended different cultures.

Covering her newly acquired bracelet as casually as possible with her other hand, Maia said, "I'm sorry. I'll be more careful next time."

* * *

THEY REMAINED IN ATHENS for the rest of the day. Maia found the city hot and crowded but still very welcoming. As the day went on, Helena peppered her with questions about any boys that may have been in the American tour group Maia had lied about, while Uncle Dorian and her grandmother had several quiet conversations that led Maia to suspect that they may not have entirely accepted her story.

On the drive home, with Helena and her grandmother asleep in the back of the car, Uncle Dorian asked Maia, "So, was the Acropolis everything you thought it might be?"

"Yes," Maia answered, as she watched the scenery go by. "I learned a lot."

CHAPTER 12

THE SILVER BRACELET

MAIA'S MOTHER CALLED the next afternoon. Maia had spent the better part of the morning in bed after telling her grandmother that she wasn't feeling well. As soon as she'd gotten home from Athens, Maia had gone straight to her room to look up the name Daedalus in her book of Greek mythology, only to find it missing. Her grandmother, who'd been keeping Maia's room fastidiously clean since her arrival, claimed not to have seen the book, though Maia was certain she'd left it in her backpack. She found only one reference to Daedalus in her Greek travel book, but it told her nothing of who he was.

As her grandmother handed her the telephone, Maia considered the consequences of letting her mother know about her experiences in the "other" Greece.

"Hi, Mom."

"Maia, sweetie! How's it going?" asked her mother with unexpected excitement.

"Okay, I guess. How's Grandpa?"

"He's doing well. He had a rough couple of days, but he's a little better now. What have you been doing?"

"Well, we went to the Acropolis yesterday. That was kind of cool," Maia stated with little commitment. "And you know, other stuff."

Maia's mother laughed, giving Maia the courage to ask, "How well did you know Uncle Dorian?"

There was a long pause on the other line. "Pretty well, I guess. Of all your father's brothers, I liked him the best. He was always good to me. Why do you ask?"

"No reason," Maia lied. She'd hoped her mother would tell her something to help her trust Uncle Dorian. "He kind of mentioned that you two were close. I was just wondering."

"Maia, are you okay?" her mother asked.

"Yeah, I'm fine. Everything's fine."

"I spoke to Adriana's mother. Adriana is going to meet you at the airport at ten o'clock on Saturday. Are you ready to come home?"

"I guess. I just wish... " Her voice trailed off and Maia finished the thought in her head. She just wished she had more time to find out why her father had to sacrifice himself to protect the "other" Greece.

"Wish what, sweetie?" her mother asked.

"I just wish the summer wasn't almost over," Maia said.

Her mother laughed again. "They'll be plenty of summer left when you get home. They finally started work on the house, and we may be able to move back in before school starts."

Maia had almost forgotten that when she got home she and her mother would still be living in Mrs. Tuttle's house. Maia heard a shuffling sound behind her, and she became aware that her grandmother had reentered the room. She was staring at the silver bracelet Maia had been given the day before. Maia turned away from her grandmother and as she did saw through a window that Uncle Dorian was walking up the path to the front door.

"Maia, are you there?" her mother asked.

"Yeah, I'm here. I was just... never mind."

"Sweetie, I have to leave for work in a few minutes. I'll call you on Friday night."

"Okay, Mom. That'll be great."

"Are you sure you're okay?"

"Yeah."

"Good. I love you."

"I love you too, Mom."

Uncle Dorian walked into the living room just as Maia hung up the telephone.

"You are out of bed? You must be feeling better."

"Yes, a little," Maia said.

Maia's grandmother spoke to her uncle in Greek.

"Oh, your mother called. I would have liked to speak to her. How are she and your grandfather?"

"They're good," Maia replied. As genuinely nice as Uncle Dorian acted, Maia didn't know if she could trust anyone. Feeling awkward, she played with her bracelet, bringing it to the attention of her uncle.

"How pretty!" said Uncle Dorian. "Where did you get your bracelet?"

"It was a gift."

Her grandmother gave her uncle an uncertain look, but Uncle Dorian just smiled. "Well, it is lovely. So, are you well enough to go for a walk with me?"

"Just the two of us?"

"Yes, I thought we could continue our talk from yesterday on the patio."

Her grandmother took Maia by the hand. "It is beautiful day. Go outside with uncle."

Maia had planned to stay home and search for her Greek mythology book, but she was curious as to what her uncle had to say, especially since the last thing they'd spoken about on the patio had been her father.

"Okay, just give me a few minutes." Maia walked to her room and shut the door behind her. She stared at the bracelet the boy she'd known as Talos had given her. Maia wondered if she could ask her uncle to tell her about Daedalus without arousing his suspicion.

Maia made one last, fruitless search for her book before grabbing a sweatshirt and stepping back into the hallway. She paused. It sounded as if her uncle and grandmother were arguing. Maia took another step. They were indeed fighting about something, but Maia couldn't understand what they were saying. She was intrigued by what Uncle Dorian, who until now had been so passive, could be arguing about with her grandmother. After a few seconds, Maia heard her grandmother slam the door to the kitchen.

Maia reached back and shut her bedroom door, hard enough for her uncle to hear in the living room, before she walked down the hallway. Her uncle was sitting in a chair holding his head in his hands. Hearing Maia enter the room, Uncle Dorian looked up and forced a smile.

"Is everything okay?" Maia asked.

"Yes, of course. Your grandmother was just pestering me about when I am going to get married."

"Oh, okay," Maia said. Uncle Dorian was a pretty good liar when pressed too.

"So, are you ready for our walk?"

"Where are we going?"

"I thought we would drive to Cape Sounion. We can visit the Temple of Poseidon and then walk down by the beach."

"What about... Yaya?" Maia asked, using the word Helena and her other cousins called her grandmother.

"She is tired from yesterday, and she is going to have dinner with your great aunt. We have the rest of the day to ourselves."

As they left the house, Maia tried to ignore the now-familiar sensation of excitement tempered by worry. After all, there was no reason why this day should feel different than any other she'd spent in Greece.

CHAPTER 13

A SON NAMED ICARUS

UNCLE DORIAN TALKED about a variety of trivial things as they made the short drive to Cape Sounion. Rather than take the initiative, Maia decided she'd wait for him to bring up the conversation about her father they'd started the day before.

"Cape Sounion is a very special place, Maia. In ancient times, it served many purposes. The Temple of Poseidon is still a magnificent sight."

"Another place where the gods once walked," Maia said quietly.

"What did you say?"

"I think I read about it in my book of Greek mythology... before it disappeared," Maia said.

"Disappeared?"

"It was in my room, but now it's gone. Yaya said she hasn't seen it."

Uncle Dorian laughed. "Your grandmother has a way of hiding things when she cleans. I will ask her about it when we get home."

"Thanks," Maia said. She paused for a moment. "Uncle Dorian, do you know a lot about mythology?"

"Some. I must admit I was never that interested. Why do you ask?"

"Do you know who Daedalus was?"

Before Uncle Dorian could answer, a car coming in the opposite direction swerved into the lane Maia and her uncle were driving in, causing Uncle Dorian to slam on the brakes and veer onto the shoulder of the road. Uncle Dorian screamed something at the other driver that didn't require translation.

"I am sorry, Maia. So many of my countrymen drive like... how do you say... lunatics, eh, crazy people."

Maia frowned. Their near-accident was awfully convenient. Was she not supposed to ask about Daedalus? After a few minutes, Uncle Dorian seemed to have regained his composure, so Maia decided to try again.

"I was wondering if you'd ever heard of Daedalus."

Her uncle didn't respond.

"Uncle Dorian?"

"Oh, Daedalus, yes. He was a craftsman... an artificer. He designed and built many things, including, if I recall correctly, the maze that held the Minotaur of myth."

Uncle Dorian suddenly seemed suspicious. "Why do you ask about Daedalus?"

"I thought I'd read something about him in my book. Was he famous for anything else?"

"For anything else? Well, yes, but mostly I think for having an idiot for a son."

Maia's eyes widened. That wasn't the response she'd expected.

"Well, here we are."

Uncle Dorian pulled into a parking spot and turned off the engine. "Come," he said with a smile, before getting out of the car.

Maia got out from the passenger side and ran to catch up with her uncle as he approached a small building.

"You wait here. I will buy our tickets."

Was it possible? Her uncle had actually made reference to Daedalus's son, whom Maia had coolly taken to calling "the boy formerly known as Talos." Maia wondered how important

Daedalus and his son were in Greek mythology. Perhaps the boy had good reason to brag about his father.

Maia looked around her. There were tourists, but not as many as on the Acropolis. It was a little warmer than the day before. Maia could smell the sea air, which reminded her once again of home. She wondered if she was being stupid not telling her mother about what had gone on in Greece… and the "other" Greece. Anyone else with a brain would probably have gotten on a plane back home right away. Although, Maia had to admit, as scared as she'd been on the Acropolis, it had been exciting as well. Until a few weeks ago, her life had been fairly boring. It was strange now to think that the only thing she'd been looking forward to this summer had been playing her guitar.

Maia kicked at the rocky ground idly as she remembered the day three years ago when her grandfather brought the guitar home for her. She'd been complaining about how much she disliked playing the flute, so Grandpa bought her a used guitar he said once belonged to a well-known Long Island musician. He told Maia that the guitar was a much cooler instrument than the flute. Her mother balked quite a bit, which was understandable considering how expensive the flute had been, so Maia had to promise to play both. She learned how to play the guitar at home while she continued practicing the flute at school. Maia agreed with Grandpa – the guitar was a much cooler instrument.

"Maia," Uncle Dorian called. "We are ready. This way."

Maia and her uncle walked up a path leading to the temple. "Wondrous, is it not?" asked Uncle Dorian.

Maia silently agreed. The Temple of Poseidon was stunning. The columns of the structure reminded her of the Parthenon, though it was much less intact. The ruins overlooked the sea, and Maia thought that in its prime the temple must have been an awe-inspiring sight. Maia listened to Uncle Dorian tell her about Cape Sounion and the role that Poseidon played in the tales of the gods. Maia thought it odd that for someone who claimed not to have much interest in mythology, Uncle Dorian knew quite a lot.

After several minutes, he asked, "So, do you like it?"

"Yes, it's amazing," Maia said. "It looks very familiar, like I've seen it from this angle before. Wait! The picture in my room... this is where—"

"Where your parents were married, yes. Your mother always said Sounion was where she and your father fell in love."

Maia imagined her mother standing in front of the temple. This place had been very special to her... until it all fell apart. Maia found herself tearing up. Bolstered by the reminder of her mother's heartbreak, Maia turned and faced her uncle, ready at last to ask him the questions she'd been reluctant to until now.

"Uncle Dorian, there's something I have to know," Maia began.

"Come, let us go down to the beach. We can get something to eat, and afterward we will walk by the water and talk."

"No, I want to talk now!"

"Maia, why are you speaking that way?" Uncle Dorian asked. "What is wrong?"

"What happened to my father?"

Uncle Dorian's face dropped. "Maia," he said, looking around uneasily, "I do not know."

"You don't know?" Maia asked. "Or you won't tell me?"

"Maia, what is this all about?"

"I heard you arguing with Yaya! I've seen the looks you give each other!"

Maia didn't like directing her anger at her uncle, but everything she'd been holding back threatened to erupt if she didn't continue.

"My mother told me she thought you were all keeping the truth from her. But now I know the truth!"

Uncle Dorian's expression changed from one of surprise to concern.

"What is it you think you know?" he asked.

"I know about the other world. I've been there! I know that my father is gone because of some promise he made. And I know that you're all still trying to keep the truth from me and my mother!"

Though still quite heated, Maia stopped her rant. Uncle Dorian no longer looked concerned. Instead, he seemed sad. Maia wasn't sure what to think of his reaction.

"Well, aren't you going to say something?"

"There is nothing for me to say. You have obviously been misinformed," Uncle Dorian said.

"Misinformed? I told you. I've been there! Yesterday, when I disappeared at the Acropolis, I wasn't with a tour group. Someone brought me to that other world, the one where the gods still exist. And it wasn't the first time. The day I arrived here, I was brought there too. Don't pretend you know nothing about this!"

"I do not have to pretend, Maia. You are not making any sense."

"No? Then what happened to my father? Why is it such a big secret?"

"I told you that I do not know what happened to him, Maia. I do not know anything about his disappearance except that he was in some kind of trouble. When my brothers and I tried to help him, he would not let us. He said he had to take care of it on his own."

"I don't believe you!"

"Maia, that is enough! I have given you no reason to doubt me. I have tried to answer your questions, but if you continue with this silly story about a place with the gods, then I cannot help you."

"You say my story about going to another world is silly? Well, then it shouldn't matter if I wear this!"

Maia gripped the silver bracelet and pulled it off her wrist.

"This was given to me in that other world to protect me. But if I'm just being silly, then I don't need it!"

Maia threw the bracelet. She watched it sail over the side of the hill to the sea below. She faced her uncle to see his reaction, but his face revealed nothing.

Maia raised her arms and turned around in a circle. "Here I am!" she yelled. "Here I am! What are you waiting for?"

Uncle Dorian reached out and grabbed Maia by the wrists, struggling to keep her from further exclamations.

"Maia, enough! I do not know why you are carrying on like this, but it must stop now! We are leaving!"

Maia pulled herself free from her uncle. "You can leave, but I'm staying here until something happens. Daedalus's son told me that the barrier between the two worlds is weaker in certain places, places like this one where the gods were worshipped."

"Daedalus's son? Who are you talking about?"

"He was at Yaya's house the day I arrived. He called himself Talos, but then yesterday he said that wasn't his real name. You said something before about Daedalus having a son."

"In mythology, Daedalus had a son named Icarus, but he... "

"He what?" Maia asked.

"He is a fool like his father," said a harsh voice from behind her. Maia shuddered. The bearded man from the Acropolis had found her again.

Uncle Dorian attempted to grab Maia's hand, but another man appeared beside him and knocked Uncle Dorian to the ground. Maia watched in shock as he fell and didn't move.

"*Here I am. What are you waiting for?*" mimicked the bearded man. "Foolish girl. Come with me!"

The bearded man reached out to grab Maia, but she managed to dodge him. Maia ran to the entrance of the site, looking for a guard or tour guide, but there was no one to be found. What had she done? Somehow she had to get the bracelet back. Desperate, she looked for a path to the beach. But before she could act, Maia found herself blocked by several men.

"No! Get away from me!" Maia yelled.

The men surrounded her. Instinctively, she raised her hand to cover her eyes just as she was met with a bright flash of light.

CHAPTER 14

FURTHER DOWN A PATH

THE MIDDLE SCHOOL MARCHING BAND was lined up in the Sea Cliff Elementary School parking lot. Maia stood among her friends, gently pressing the keys on her flute. From somewhere in the crowd of parents and other family members that surrounded the band, Maia heard a voice call her name.

"Mom?" Maia responded. "Mom, is that you?"

"Maia, come here now!" her mother called.

Maia couldn't see her mother, but she answered her none-theless. "Mom, I can't. The parade is about to start."

Maia's band teacher called the students to order. The students began their procession out of the parking lot, heading in the direction of Sea Cliff Avenue.

"Maia, come back!" her mother's voice called again.

"Mom, I'll see you when the parade is over."

It looked like the entire town had come out to see the parade. The sidewalks of Sea Cliff Avenue were lined with people all the way down to Memorial Park.

"Maia! Maia, over here!" called someone from in front of the town hall. Maia nearly dropped her flute. It was Grandpa! He was out of the hospital and looked healthier than she could ever remember. Maia wanted to run to him, but knew she'd be in trouble with her band teacher if she did.

"Maia, look this way!" Her grandfather was holding a camera. As he took her picture, the camera let off an unusually bright flash of light. Maia flinched but kept marching. A little farther up the street, another person in the crowd took Maia's picture, again blinding her momentarily with an unusually bright light. And then another person took a picture. And another person. In all of the confusion, Maia was surprised to see that the band had marched all the way down to the harbor. The drum major was leading the band onto the beach and into the water.

"This is crazy," Maia said to no one in particular. None of the other band members appeared to care that they were headed straight for the water. The sea began to bubble furiously. From out of the harbor rose the sea god Triton holding his conch shell. He parted the water with his hand, allowing the band to continue their march into the sea. The beach was filled with spectators, all holding cameras. Again and again, flashes of bright light blinded Maia.

"Stop!" Maia yelled. "I can't see! Please!"

Maia tried to stop marching, but the other students wouldn't let her.

"Maia!" her mother called out from the crowd. "Maia, don't go!"

"Mom, where are you? I don't want to go! Please, don't let him take me!"

Maia strained to see her mother in the crowd, but the flashes of light made it impossible. She felt her feet sinking into the wet sand as she continued marching into the sea.

"I don't want to go!" Maia yelled, but her voice was drowned out by the music of the band and the cheers of the spectators. With each step, Maia felt herself sinking deeper into the sand until she couldn't move any farther. Blinded by the nonstop bright flashes of light, Maia begged for help as the sand and water threatened to consume her.

"Please, someone help me!"

Suddenly, a hand reached out, grabbed Maia, and pulled her from the wet sand – and out of her dream onto a cold, wooden floor.

"Quiet!" ordered the bearded man with the gravelly voice. "If you do not keep quiet, so help me, Lord Zeus, I will—"

"Aeton! That is enough!" said a deep voice, from the shadows. "Our lord will be displeased if you do anything further to harm her."

The man called Aeton turned and spat. "Then you watch her, Kastor! I am not a nursemaid!" Aeton brushed past Maia and exited the room through a large, wooden door. Strangely, it felt as though the room swayed slightly as he left. Maia turned in the direction of the voice of the man called Kastor.

"Are you hurt?" Kastor asked.

Maia was afraid to respond.

"I asked if you are hurt. Aeton can be rather rough."

"I-I'm fine," Maia managed to stammer.

"That is good. I am very glad to hear that."

Maia looked down. She was wearing a tunic and sandals again. She thought back to when she'd first met the boy she'd known as Talos (though perhaps his name was Icarus) and how disturbing it was to be in different clothing. Maia wanted to ask Kastor why she was there, but in truth she feared the answer, especially if the crow had told the truth. There was a war looming and somehow she was connected.

"It is a shame, really," Kastor said. "Such a shame that you had to become involved in this. After all, your father... " Kastor paused and let out a long, raspy breath. "Your father should have been enough."

Kastor leaned forward from his chair in the shadows, placing his hands on his knees. Maia could see that he was rather overweight. With some effort, Kastor brought himself to his feet and lumbered across the room. Watching him move so unsteadily, Maia thought she might be able to overtake him if given the chance. Kastor reached into a cabinet from which he pulled a bottle and a large cup and poured himself a drink.

"Where am I?" Maia asked.

Kastor chortled. "Well, child, that depends on whom you ask. To most inhabitants, it is simply Greece. It is their home and the only one they have ever known." Kastor took a large gulp of his drink before continuing. "But there are those of us... " Kastor hiccupped. "Those of us that know what the gods did call this place Olympia – the salvation of the gods. Tell me, child, are you impressed by what the gods have created here?"

"No," Maia replied with little hesitation.

Kastor let out a loud, hearty laugh. "Honesty! I admire that," he said. He took another gulp of his drink as he stumbled back to his chair.

"Still, it must seem an amazing place. From what I understand, the people of your world have long forgotten the wonderment of flying beasts and giants that can crush mountains. The gods of Olympus are no longer worshipped, and their many deeds, great and otherwise, have been all but lost to history."

Maia watched Kastor carefully. She couldn't tell if he regretted the status of the gods back home or not.

"Do you think the people of your world need to be reminded of how things once were, child? Do you think our two worlds need to become one?"

Kastor's questions surprised Maia. Was he being serious? Kastor fixed his bloodshot eyes upon her and after a moment smiled rather broadly, stifling a belch.

"After all, that is what this is all about. After many centuries of isolation, there are those who want the barrier that separates our worlds broken down. They believe the time is right for the gods to be worshipped again in your world."

"Wh-why?" Maia stammered. "Why now?"

"Those that have been allowed to make the journey have told tales of a people that have lost their sense of wonder... their sense of awe at the might of gods." Kastor swirled his drink. "Of course, child, there are those who fear the gods will make the same mistakes as before and quite possibly end up destroying themselves."

Kastor coughed, and Maia could smell something on his breath that reminded her of when her grandfather came home from meeting up with his old buddies from work. He continued, "After the Great War, which came to be known in your world as the Trojan War, the gods felt themselves growing weak. Fighting for their very survival, they made a very bold move. They used all their remaining strength and power, and indeed some made the ultimate sacrifice, to create Olympia.

"But as is often the case with the gods, the creation of Olympia was not without dissension. Though the majority of the gods survived, some were displeased. After centuries of discord that threatened to destroy all that the gods had built here, it was decided that someone would be sent back to your world. This was not an easy task, even for the gods. Olympia had been created in such a way that even they could not weaken the barrier between the two worlds enough to have someone cross over."

"That doesn't seem to be a problem now."

"Thanks to one man. In the end, it was the artificer, Daedalus, who made it possible. Once he came up with the solution, it was clear there was only one man who could lead the journey."

Kastor stopped and stared at Maia.

"Your father was given the responsibility of deciding the fate of Olympia. He was to live among the people of your world and to return when he had learned enough of their ways. But when the time came, he did not want to return. He had fallen in love, and he had a daughter with whom he did not want to part."

"But why wouldn't he take us with him?"

"Why? Because the gods would never have allowed it of course! Your father had responsibilities to reassume in Olympia. But in the end, your father's opinion did not matter. A decision had already been made. Lord Zeus, father and king of gods and man, had decreed that the two worlds would not be joined. It was then, faced with the prospect of losing you and your mother, that your father tried to turn his back on this world."

Kastor finished his drink and allowed the cup to fall to the floor. "Your father was of course brought back to Olympia and duly punished for defying the gods."

"What about my grandmother? And the rest of my family?"

"They are," Kastor said, casually waving his hand, "no longer of any consequence."

Maia didn't want to hear anymore. Kastor had spoken of her father's end so casually. She pulled at the ropes binding her, loosening them a bit, but Kastor didn't appear to notice.

"This leaves you, child. The gods have been interested in you for a very long time. Once they learned of your existence, they realized how valuable you could be... both sides did, in fact."

"*Both* sides?"

Kastor laughed. "Just because Lord Zeus had made a decree did not mean that everyone agreed with it. Indeed not. There has been a war brewing for many years now, with gods on each side."

"And where do I fit in?" asked Maia.

"You? Why, you are at the very heart of the matter, child of two worlds," Kastor said. "Without you—"

Kastor was interrupted by the opening of the large, wooden door. Aeton stood in the doorway. "We are here. Get to your feet!" he ordered.

"No," said Maia.

"What? I said get to your feet!" Aeton shouted.

"No!" shouted Maia in return.

Aeton stormed over to her. Maia kicked out her legs, sending a chair sailing toward him.

"Calm yourselves!" pleaded Kastor. "This will serve no purpose."

Aeton knocked over the chair and grabbed Maia by the hair.

"Do not make this any more difficult then it has to be!" he warned her.

Maia winced in pain as Aeton attempted to pull her to her feet by her hair.

"Please! This is not necessary," Kastor protested again. "Maia, you must cooperate!"

Maia continued to struggle, which only caused Aeton to pull harder. She looked to Kastor, but it was obvious he wasn't going to move against Aeton. Finally, she stood. Aeton grabbed her by the arm and shoved her through the doorway. Maia heard other voices shouting orders. Aeton pushed her down a long, narrow hallway, and then forced her to climb a ladder leading to an opening on the deck of a ship. The men on board were busy tying the ship to a dock. They'd been sailing away from Cape Sounion the entire time Kastor had been telling his drunken tale.

"This way!" Aeton shouted, pushing Maia over the side of the ship and onto the dock. Maia turned around to see Kastor struggling to climb out of the hatch.

Aeton led Maia off the dock to a wagon nearby and pushed her aboard.

"Take us to the castle!" Aeton commanded the driver.

Maia looked in all directions. In the distance, beyond the front of the wagon, she thought she could see a castle on a hill.

"Wait for me! Aeton, wait!" called Kastor, from the deck of the ship. Panting heavily, he climbed onto the dock and followed the road to the wagon. After Kastor climbed aboard, Aeton motioned to the driver. Maia's stomach lurched as the wagon sped off toward the castle. Whoever lived within its walls was certain to draw her further down a path her father had already traveled.

CHAPTER 15

MORE THAN ONE THING PERHAPS

THE ROAD TO THE CASTLE was long and rough. Aeton had tied Maia's hands to a post in the back of the wagon, and under his watchful eye Maia saw no opportunity to attempt an escape. She wondered about the castle and who lived there. Speaking to Aeton on the ship, Kastor had made reference to someone as "our lord." The castle could belong to him, she guessed. Regardless of his intentions for her, she hoped that he was more gentle than Aeton and less befuddled than Kastor.

Looking back at the water, Maia could see the setting sun. Several hours must have passed since she'd been with Uncle Dorian on Cape Sounion. The passage of time appeared to be the same in Olympia as at home, so Maia worried that word would have gotten to her mother about her disappearance by now. Her lip trembled at the thought of her mother receiving a phone call from Uncle Dorian. How would she react? Would she get on an airplane and come to Greece? It wouldn't matter. Her mother was no more able to rescue her than anyone else back home.

After some time, the wagon slowed, and Aeton started barking orders at the driver again. Maia looked over at Kastor, who appeared to be having a difficult time with the journey – or more likely with what he'd consumed back on the ship.

The wagon came to a stop. Maia pulled at her ropes, but Aeton was at her side within seconds. "That's enough!" he told her, grabbing Maia by the hair with one hand as he loosened the rope tying her to the post with the other. He let go of her hair only to grab her by the arm and pull her off the wagon. Kastor remained in his spot holding his head in his hands. Maia thought he was going to be sick.

"Kastor, you imbecile, get up!" Aeton shouted.

Maia got her first look at the castle. It was larger than she'd thought. Lights were burning in some of the windows, but the castle was otherwise dark and unwelcoming. It had none of the splendor of the Parthenon or Temple of Poseidon.

"I said get up!"

Groaning, Kastor stood. After taking one unsteady step, he managed a spectacular fall off the wagon onto the rocky ground.

"You are pathetic," Aeton said. "Driver, see that my portly companion is not injured. Come, girl! There's a cell waiting for you."

Grabbing a torch from the driver, Aeton led Maia to the rear of the castle. They stopped before a large, wooden door with wrought iron spikes. Aeton held Maia with a firm grip as he knocked loudly on the door.

From the other side came a voice. "Who is it?"

"Open the door, fool! I have the girl!"

Maia flinched. She knew she couldn't let Aeton take her inside. As the door opened, Maia grabbed for the torch, bringing it down onto Aeton's head. He jumped back, allowing Maia to break free from his grip. She sprinted away from the castle without knowing where to go. Not far in front of her, there appeared to be a wooded area. She could hide there, but then what? She had no way of reaching anyone in her own world, and she doubted that Daedalus's son would come and rescue her. As far as he knew, Maia was safe wearing her bracelet.

Maia was several yards away from the woods when she heard Kastor call out to her.

"Stop! There are creatures in those woods that would not take kindly to your presence," the large man warned. "They are unlikely to attack anyone outside the woods, but should someone enter... "

Maia stopped at the edge of what she could now see was an expansive forest. Even without Kastor's warning, Maia knew she shouldn't go any farther. Something was watching her. More than one thing perhaps. Maia took one tentative step back, then another, and prepared to break into a run again, this time heading for the road. But before she could cover any real ground, someone came charging at her from the direction of the castle. She felt a searing pain in the back of her head – and everything went black.

CHAPTER 16

DIRECTED BY A GOD

"HERE, YOU MUST TRY to eat something," said a high-pitched voice.

Maia's head throbbed with pain. Just the thought of opening her eyes hurt.

"Eat this. It will make you feel better."

With some effort, Maia raised her head in the direction of the voice and gradually opened her eyes. There was a girl, perhaps no older than Maia herself, kneeling beside her holding a spoon containing a hot, thick liquid.

"This will help ease your pain. Father is very angry with Aeton for hitting you with that stone. He is such a savage."

Maia took in her surroundings. She was in a cell of cold, damp stone and iron fittings with loose hay scattered about. From her position kneeling on the hard floor with her arms and legs bound behind her, Maia spied a small window with bars high up in the wall.

"Come now. Open your mouth," the girl insisted.

Maia allowed the girl to place the spoon in her mouth and was amazed to feel her headache dissipating even as the liquid went down her throat. She looked at the girl beside her. She too was wearing a tunic and sandals, but Maia could see that they were of much better quality and design than her own. The girl also wore her hair in a very elaborate style. Maia's eyes met hers, and the girl gave Maia a sympathetic, if unconvincing, smile.

"Father only uses Aeton because he always accomplishes what Father tells him to do, even if his methods are somewhat brutal," the girl said, as she offered Maia another spoonful. "That is why Kastor is assigned to keep an eye on him," she continued.

"Who is your father?" Maia asked, as she gulped down the miraculous liquid.

"Why, my father is King Alphaios. And I am his daughter, Princess Akantha."

"My name is—"

"Oh, you do not have to tell me your name, Maia. I know who you are," the princess said with a mischievous smile. "Soon, everyone will know who you are."

"What do you mean?" Maia asked.

"There is a feast to be held in honor of your arrival. Preparations are all under way, and by this evening all of Father's guests should have arrived. I heard Father say that one of *them* may be coming as well!" Akantha said.

"Who are *them*?" Maia asked.

"Why, the gods, of course," Akantha whispered. "Now, hurry. You must finish this. There will be no more food for you until the feast."

By now the pain had all but subsided, but Maia did as she was told. It wasn't as if she had much choice. Hopeful that Akantha could prove to be an ally, Maia chose her words very carefully.

"Are you going to the feast?"

"Of course I am. As the king's daughter, I will have a seat right by his side."

"And what about me?"

"You? Well, I suppose there will be a seat for you somewhere. Not next to Father, obviously."

"Are all of the guests being kept in cells?" Maia asked.

"What? Of course not! How could you ask such a stupid question?"

"Then why am I here?"

"Because it is as Father wishes," Akantha answered, forcing another spoonful into Maia's mouth.

Maia gulped the liquid down as she plotted how to get the conversation on a track that would leave her with better options.

"You know who I am," Maia stated casually.

"Yes, we have already determined that."

"So then, you know where I come from."

"Really, do you not have anything else to speak of but yourself? It is rather boring."

Maia rolled her eyes. The girl was really thick.

"Akantha, if you know where I come from then you also know that I don't belong here. You have to help me escape."

"Escape?" Akantha repeated, a look of horror on her small, bony face. "How could you suggest that I would help you do such a thing? After everything Father has done to ensure your safe arrival, you would repay him by trying to escape?"

"Do you call being tossed around by my hair by that animal Aeton part of my safe arrival?" Maia asked, struggling to accept that anyone could be so dense. "Akantha, I don't know what you or anyone else has been told about me, but I want to go home!"

Akantha stood, a cold, haughty expression upon her face. With her nose pointed upward, she said, "You do not deserve any more of my help. You are so ungrateful! I shall tell Father to send Aeton back here. Perhaps he does know best how to deal with you."

Akantha grabbed the small, black cauldron containing the miraculous liquid that had cured Maia's headache and a dozen other assorted pains, and she marched to the door of the cell.

Knocking sharply, Akantha scowled at Maia as she waited for the door to be opened for her.

"To think, I had hoped we would be friends," Akantha said, annoyed that Maia wasn't grateful for her attention. The door opened and Akantha stormed out, leaving a bewildered Maia alone in the cell.

"What is it with the kids in this place and their fathers?" Maia mumbled. She strained to turn and face the small window high in the wall opposite the door. Through the bars, she could make out the early light of morning. She'd slept through the night.

"If there really are gods, maybe one of you will take pity on me and get me out of this mess," Maia said loudly, looking up at the window. She tried pulling at her binds. Grateful not to be in chains, Maia allowed herself a glimmer of hope. Out of the corner of her eye, Maia spotted a large mouse as it scrambled for food in the corner of the cell. Though typically not afraid of such things, her initial surprise at seeing the mouse was enough to cause Maia to lose her balance and send her onto her side.

In spite of her circumstances, Maia allowed herself a small smile. She remembered when she and her friend Jacqueline had tried to reenact an escape artist trick after reading a story in school about Harry Houdini. Their attempt ended with both of them tied to a tree in Memorial Park. Luckily, they were able to persuade Jacqueline's brother Samuel to go for help.

"Grandpa's not going to come running with a hacksaw this time," Maia told herself. As she attempted to put herself upright, Maia felt something furry brush against her wrist, and she let out a yelp. Just the idea of the mouse looking at her as its next meal sent a wave of disgust through her. Maia rolled onto her other side as she tried to loosen the ropes binding her wrists. The mouse was watching her. It made its way over to Maia's side, stopping a few inches from her face. Even as Maia kicked and rolled on the ground, the mouse remained in its place.

"Get away!" Maia shouted.

After several futile attempts on Maia's part to free herself, she gave up. The mouse hadn't moved and was still looking in her direction. "Okay, mouse," Maia said, "you stay on your side of the cell, and I'll stay on mine."

The mouse lifted itself onto its back legs and, staring Maia in the eyes, shook its head. The mouse scrambled its way around Maia, who was now lying on her front with her feet and hands bound above her. Maia could only lay there whimpering as the mouse crawled up her arm to her wrist and began chewing on the ropes.

Maia tried to turn her head to watch the mouse. With some difficulty, she came to terms with the fact that the mouse was trying to help her. Recalling that the last time she was in Olympia she'd been helped by a boy on a winged horse and a pair of crows, Maia decided to focus on the rescue, not the rescuer.

"You're not going to make fun of my clothes too, are you?"

The mouse paused for a moment, looked Maia up and down, and turned its head to the side before going back to work. As she lay there, with little else to think about other than escape, Maia tried to figure out where her cell might be located in the castle. A dungeon was a likely choice, but Maia wasn't sure what to make of the window and the height of the walls. Once she was free, the window would be too high to reach anyway, and she doubted she'd get very far in the castle if she were able to get out through the door.

While the mouse continued to chew through the ropes, Maia thought back to what Akantha had said. An actual Greek god was supposed to attend the feast. Maia wondered what interest a god could have in her, even if she were a "child of two worlds." In almost all of the Greek myths Maia had read, the gods did little more than cause problems for mortal men and women. Both Icarus and Kastor had said that Olympia had been created solely because the gods had crossed their followers too many times. Maia couldn't understand why some of the gods would ever want to rejoin this world with hers. They would put themselves at risk again. Worse still, the people of her world would be in jeopardy from their meddling.

Maia felt the ropes binding her hands come loose. "Way to go, little guy!" Maia exclaimed. She turned over and started to untie her feet. The mouse watched Maia carefully, seemingly unimpressed with her efforts.

"What? You think you could do a better job?" Maia asked.

The mouse lifted itself onto its back legs and nodded its head. It scampered off into the corner of the cell and disappeared into a small hole in the wall.

"Thanks," Maia called to the mouse. A few minutes later, Maia was free of the ropes. She stood and walked over to the wall with the high window, but she couldn't see much. Maia moved toward the door. Leaning against it, she couldn't hear anything on the other side. Instead, a voice came from the window.

"You should not have removed the bracelet."

Maia clenched her teeth. Turning around, she found herself again, as on the afternoon of her arrival in Greece, facing the boy whose goofy grin so perplexed her. He smiled uncertainly at her as he gripped the bars of the window.

"What are you doing here?" Maia asked. "How did you find me?"

"News of your arrival spread very quickly. King Alphaios has been dispatching messengers throughout the night to ensure that the feast in your honor is well attended. It is said that the gods themselves will send an envoy."

"Icarus – that is your name, right?" Without waiting for a reply, Maia continued. "I don't care if Elvis himself is providing the entertainment. I don't plan on attending a feast."

"I do not know anyone by the name of Elvis, but you are correct. My name is Icarus. I apologize for the deception, but I did not know if you had heard of me."

"Heard of you?" Maia asked with contempt. "No, I've never heard of you, but I'll ask the mayor of Sea Cliff to erect a statue of you in front of town hall if you get me out of here."

"I am working on a solution to that problem as we speak."

"No offense, Icarus, but why isn't your father here? Isn't he the great inventor?"

"My father has other matters with which to contend," Icarus said, blushing. "He is greatly displeased that you are here once again. I should have ensured that you did not return."

"Icarus, that wasn't your fault," Maia said. "I got myself into this mess. I was taunting my uncle, and I threw the bracelet away. If I'd listened to you, I'd be back at my grandmother's house right now, instead of here, trapped in a cell."

"Still, we must return you to your world." Glancing around the cell, Icarus asked, "How did you free yourself from the ropes?"

"I had help. As crazy as it sounds, a mouse showed up and chewed through most of them." Maia smirked. "I know it doesn't make sense. Maybe I'm still a little loopy from being hit on the head."

Icarus laughed. "After all that you have seen here, is it still so incredible that a mouse would act in such a way? The mouse was being directed by a god. Which one, I do not know. But this is a good sign. We have divine intervention on our side."

"Well, from everything I've heard, divine intervention isn't always what it's cracked up to be."

Maia heard movement outside of the door to the cell.

"Someone's coming!"

"Maia, I will return. Do not do anything to provoke your captors," Icarus whispered before he disappeared from the window.

Maia dove to the corner of the cell, grabbing the remains of the ropes and thrusting her hands behind her. She waited for the door to open, hoping to see Akantha, as she was eager to show the princess what she thought of her now that her hands were free. Maia's heart dropped as Aeton entered the room, leaving the door open behind him.

"So, you asked the king's daughter to help you escape?" Aeton spat. "Foolish little girl."

As Aeton approached Maia, he noticed the bits of rope on the floor of the cell.

"What is this? Have you actually been trying to free yourself, you foul creature?" Aeton raced to the corner where Maia kneeled and raised his fist to strike her. Maia felt a rustling behind her as the mouse that had chewed through her ropes charged Aeton along with several dozen other mice, repeatedly biting his feet and legs. Aeton let out a furious shriek and swatted in vain at the mice as they continued their attack.

Maia jumped to her feet and ran past Aeton out of the cell. Perhaps Icarus had been right about divine intervention. It was proving to be more and more promising. From back in the cell, Maia could hear a string of curses that would even make her grandfather blush.

"So much for not provoking my captors," Maia said to herself, as she ran down a hallway leading to a spiral staircase. As she bounded down the stairs, Maia reasoned that her cell was at the top of a tower. Had Icarus been riding Pierinos when he appeared at the window of the cell?

Maia's thoughts were interrupted as she exited the staircase into another long hallway. She wasn't alone. Maia could hear voices at the other end of the hallway, including one that was annoyingly familiar. Maia took two steps back up the stairs and crouched down to listen.

"No, Father! I will not help her prepare for the feast!" Akantha protested. "She is horrible!"

"Now, now, my daughter," Akantha's father, King Alphaios responded. "You will do as your father asks. Otherwise, I know you will be very disappointed to miss our guest."

"It is not fair!" Akantha continued, "I do not want to share my clothing with her. She is a commoner."

"A *commoner*? Dear daughter, you have not listened to your father. That girl is much more than a commoner. She is—"

"She is dead when I am through with her," Aeton interrupted. Maia hadn't realized that the bearded man had come up behind her until it was too late. Aeton grabbed Maia by the neck and pulled her out of the stairwell and down the hallway toward the surprised king and his ill-tempered daughter. As they got closer, Maia could see a smile forming on Akantha's otherwise hard face.

"She tried to escape," said Aeton. "She got free of her ropes and set a trap for me when I entered her cell."

"See Father, I told you!" Akantha exclaimed with more than a little obvious satisfaction.

Aeton threw Maia to the ground. She landed on her hands and knees in front of King Alphaios. Maia nearly winced, but caught herself. She didn't want to give Aeton or Akantha the pleasure of seeing her in pain.

"That is enough! From both of you!" commanded King Alphaios, looking from Aeton to Akantha. The king extended his hand to Maia. "I am sorry for how you have been treated."

Maia took the king's hand and stood. She looked in his eyes, which to her surprise were kind and reassuring.

"To attempt an escape. How resourceful," King Alphaios said with apparent curiosity. "Just like your father."

Two guards appeared behind the king. Maia felt Akantha glaring at her, but as benevolent as King Alphaios seemed, she dared not glare back.

"Aeton, you may go," King Alphaios told him.

"But your highness, she is quite—" Aeton protested.

"Go," the king ordered.

Grumbling to himself, Aeton turned and stomped down the hallway.

"Now, if we have no further matters to discuss, my daughter will take you to her chambers and help you prepare for the feast," said the king.

Maia nodded, her expression neutral.

"Oh, come on," Akantha said through gritted teeth. She took Maia by the hand and pulled her past the king and down the hallway escorted by the two guards.

"Yes," Maia could hear the king say, as she was pulled along by Akantha, "so much like her father."

CHAPTER 17

SOMETHING WITH GREAT FINALITY

"HONESTLY, I DO NOT KNOW what Father is thinking," said Akantha, as she stormed about a large sitting room in her chambers. "She does not deserve a feast. She does not deserve anything."

Akantha flopped down on a pile of overstuffed pillows.

"She certainly does not deserve an audience with one of them. Not even I have met one of the gods," said Akantha, as she stared dreamily through a nearby window.

Maia stood in the doorway of Akantha's sitting room, listening to the princess's tirade. It had gone on for at least twenty minutes, and Maia was beginning to feel nostalgic for her cell.

"Tell me!" Akantha commanded, addressing Maia directly for the first time since King Alphaios had dismissed them. "Where you come from, are the daughters of kings treated with so much dis-respect that they are made to dress... someone such as you?"

Maia stammered, "I d-don't know. I h-haven't met many princesses before."

All at once, Akantha brightened. "You have not? Well then, are you impressed?"

Maia tried to keep a straight face. As difficult as the position she found herself in was, bringing herself to shower Akantha with praise wasn't going to be an easy task.

"Well, are you impressed by me?" Akantha asked again, her eyes narrowed.

"Y-yes, of course I am," Maia said. "You are so b-beautiful, and... your clothes are, are, um, divine."

Akantha lifted her chin and pursed her lips. "Perhaps I was wrong about you."

The princess rose gracefully from the bed of pillows and pranced over to a large gilded mirror. "There is much I could teach you, Maia. I do not think you could ever look as heavenly as I, but yes, I could teach you many things."

As Akantha surveyed herself in the mirror, Maia struggled to keep her composure. Glancing around the room, Maia wondered how much more trouble she would be in if she smothered Akantha with one of the countless pillows. Oblivious to Maia's aggressive thoughts, Akantha continued to chatter away.

"They are coming from all over for the feast. Father sent messengers far and wide. I must look my very best." Akantha added, "And we will have to find something for you too, I suppose. I cannot let Father think that I did not try."

Akantha looked Maia up and down. "When was the last time you even washed your hair?"

Maia was still eyeing the pillows when she was struck with a less deadly thought. Performing her best impression of her cousin Helena, Maia asked, "So, will there be any boys at the feast?"

"Boys?" Akantha repeated, as she turned away from the mirror. "Oh yes! Though probably not the one I long most to see. Not since his father and my father had a disagreement."

"Oh, I'm so sorry to hear that," Maia offered with as much fake empathy as she could muster. "What's his name?"

"I really should not tell you," Akantha said, her haughty expression returning. "Father does not even like his or his father's name mentioned within the walls of the castle. Still, after tonight, it will not matter what you know, so... "

Before Maia could ask Akantha what she meant by that quip, the princess flounced over to her and pulled her to the center of the room, throwing Maia atop a pile of pillows.

"His name is Icarus, and he is ever so clever," Akantha boasted. "The first time I met him, I thought he was rather ordinary. But then he spoke to me of such wondrous things, of places and creatures that I do not think Father would ever let me see."

Maia remained silent. The revelation of Akantha's relationship with Icarus was small compared to the possibility that something with great finality was going to happen to her after tonight.

Akantha continued, "Father never wants me to leave the castle. He says it is too dangerous, but I long for the possibility of journeying to different places. Icarus will come for me one day. I know he will."

Akantha caught her reflection in the mirror and smiled. Maia considered whether to ask her for an explanation of what was to take place after the feast, but the words wouldn't come. After a while, Akantha stopped admiring herself long enough to notice that Maia was troubled.

"Is there something wrong? Are you not happy for me, or are you so self-obsessed that you cannot look beyond your own fate?" Akantha asked, placing her hands on her hips.

"What do you mean by fate?" Maia asked. "What's going to happen to me tonight?"

Akantha let out a small huff. "Tonight, if all goes well, Father will have his way. The gods will be appeased, and all talk of war will end."

"But what does that have to do with me?" Maia asked, her voice rising with her growing distress.

"How dare you speak to me like that?" The princess glared at Maia. "You are to be sacrificed. That is all I know," Akantha stated, her arms crossed in indignation.

Maia was stunned, not only by Akantha's words, but by the heartless manner in which they were delivered.

"How can you just stand there and talk about my being sacrificed as if you were talking about choosing a new set of clothes?" Maia asked.

Akantha snorted and turned away from Maia.

There was a knock at the door, and an older woman in white robes entered the room.

"Your highness, the king wishes to see you," said the woman.

"I will be there momentarily," answered Akantha, waving the woman away. She looked at Maia after the woman left the room. "There is nothing I can do for you."

Akantha walked over to the mirror and examined her reflection again. After a full minute, she turned and went to the door.

"Do not touch anything until I return," Akantha ordered before leaving.

Maia ran her hands through her bushy hair as she allowed herself to take in the full meaning of Akantha's words. They weren't going to let her go home when this was all over. Maia stood and walked in a circle, wringing her hands as she took in small gasps of breath.

"This c-can't be h-happening," Maia stammered, her words catching in her throat. "I don't b-belong here. I don't belong here, and I want to go home!"

Maia paced around the edge of the room over and over again before stopping in front of a window.

"Icarus! Icarus, I need your help!" Maia cried out the window. "Please! Someone help me!"

Maia crumbled to the floor, more frightened than she'd ever been in her thirteen years.

CHAPTER 18

IF ALL GOES WELL

MAIA'S PLEAS ASIDE, Icarus hadn't come, and the rest of the morning and afternoon passed slowly but uneventfully. Upon her return, Akantha continued to bemoan her own fate as to having been assigned to dress Maia for the feast. Maia said nothing as Akantha tossed assorted garments about the room and treated Maia to tales of stolen moments and secret getaways with Icarus.

"He wanted to know everything about me," Akantha gushed. "We explored every corner of this castle – just the two of us."

Maia ducked as a long, white gown with gold trim flew by her head.

"Still," Akantha continued, "I would have preferred to hear more about what life is like away from this island. Icarus has been to so many remarkable places. He says he has even been to the great games held in honor of the gods!"

Maia did her best to ignore Akantha as she prattled on. Not knowing what else to do, Maia tried on several of the outfits Akantha threw her way. With each fitting, Akantha bombarded Maia with criticism while praising her own beauty and sense of style. The afternoon slipped into evening. After countless fittings, Akantha conceded that Maia didn't look horrible in a particular gown of red and gold, and she set upon tending to Maia's hair.

"I do not think I have ever seen such an unwieldy mess in all my life!" Akantha remarked. "Father will just have to understand that there is nothing more I can do."

Maia looked at herself in the mirror. In addition to tying Maia's hair back in braids and adding a jeweled headpiece, Akantha had applied a generous amount of makeup. In spite of Akantha's protests and Maia's general aversion to eye shadow, lipstick, and blush, Maia had to concede that, even if she wasn't emotionally prepared for an audience with a god, she was at least somewhat physically appropriate.

"Oh!" Akantha suddenly exclaimed. "Look at the hour! We should have left some time ago."

Akantha ran around the room nearly tripping over the many pillows and discarded dresses. She paused in front of a mirror to bite her lips and pinch her cheeks to bring color to her face. Maia was surprised to see Akantha so panic-stricken, and, despite her misery, it took tremendous effort for Maia not to smile.

"Why are you still sitting there?" Akantha asked in exasperation. "We must go now!"

Akantha grabbed Maia by the wrist and pulled her through her chambers out into a long hallway. A guard appeared in front of them, blocking their path.

"Your highness, the king has asked that you remain in your quarters," the guard told Akantha. "Your guest is to remain there as well until she is summoned."

"Nonsense!" cried Akantha. "We are to attend the feast. My father—"

"Told you to stay in your quarters," interrupted the guard. "I was there when he gave you the order."

"It is unfair!" Akantha shouted, stamping her foot. "First he tells me that I must prepare this commoner for the feast, and then he tells me I cannot attend."

Maia watched the exchange between Akantha and the guard with growing amusement. Akantha reminded her of too many girls in her grade at school, always angry with their parents for failing to meet one unrealistic expectation or another. Maia wondered how long it would take Akantha to lapse into a full-blown temper tantrum.

Before Maia's prediction could come to pass, another guard came charging down the hallway.

"Ophelos, it is time!" said the second guard.

The guard named Ophelos turned to Akantha. "Your highness, I implore you to return to your quarters."

Akantha stamped her foot again but said nothing.

"You," Ophelos said, as he turned to Maia, "will come with me."

The second guard stayed behind with Akantha as Ophelos led Maia down the hallway. Akantha's cries of "It is unfair!" echoed through the halls as they navigated their way through the castle.

Maia resigned herself to being at the mercy of others. She could no longer rely on Icarus or anyone else to save her. "You are to be sacrificed," Akantha had said. Just like her father, Maia thought.

Ophelos brought Maia before a large set of wooden doors. On each side stood a guard.

"The king is expecting us," Ophelos stated.

One of the guards nodded and opened the doors. Maia felt the guard's eyes on her as she passed through the doorway. Did every-one in the castle know what was going to happen to her?

Instead of the banquet hall Maia expected after Akantha's rant-ing about a feast, she'd been led into King Alphaios's throne room. The king was seated before a pair of excitable young men who were peppering him with questions.

"Yes, yes, that is all fine," King Alphaios said, waving the men away. "There is nothing that can be changed now that will make any sizeable difference. Now go! I will not be late for a feast I myself am hosting."

The two young men bowed to the king, turned, and hurried past Maia and Ophelos.

"Ah! My dear child," said King Alphaios, taking notice of Maia. "Come, let me look at you."

Ophelos nudged Maia, and, heavy-footed, she walked to where the king was seated.

"My daughter treated you well, I presume? She certainly shared some of her gift for stylishness with you," King Alphaios said warmly.

Still hesitant but slowly gaining her composure, Maia wondered how the king would react if he knew that the princess had shared much more than just beauty tips.

"Guard, give us a moment," King Alphaios directed.

"Yes, your highness," Ophelos responded. "I will be outside the doors."

The king continued to look at Maia and smile. After Ophelos had left the room, he said, "My guard is concerned about your resourcefulness."

Maia swallowed, afraid there would be consequences of her mouse-assisted escape.

"Tell me, Maia. Do you know why you are here?"

Maia cast her eyes downward and shifted from foot to foot before responding. "To be sacrificed."

"Sacrificed?" the king repeated. "From where would you derive such a foolish notion?"

Maia lifted her head and looked directly at King Alphaios for the first time since entering the throne room. She was relieved to see that he was still smiling.

"Perhaps my daughter would like to hope that you are to be sacrificed – she simply cannot bear the competition," King Alphaios said, fairly amused. "No, Maia, you are far too important. If all goes well, you will return to your home this very evening, after your presence here has served its purpose."

"What purpose is that?" Maia asked.

"To demonstrate to the nonbelievers that your world is worthy of being joined with ours. Can you not see? In you, lies the proof."

King Alphaios took note of the puzzled look on Maia's face.

"You are a smart girl. Surely, by now you have pieced some things together. I know for a fact that Kastor kept you well entertained on the ride over from the mainland. Very well entertained, I suppose. Kastor does like his drink."

King Alphaios stood and approached Maia.

"No harm will come to you, I promise. Some of my guests this evening would prefer you did not exist, but they will not act against my wishes. In exchange for your safe return home, I ask only one thing – that you answer any question asked of you *honestly*."

"Who is going to be asking me questions?"

"Maia, you and your world are of great interest to those who know of your existence. When your father was sent forth to judge the wisdom of rejoining our two worlds, no one would have predicted the outcome. Your father held an unimaginable position of power. That he above all would forsake this world caused many of us to question our own beliefs. I myself was a dissenter. Leading up to your father's return, I was certain that our worlds should forever be kept apart."

King Alphaios paced the throne room, more animated with every step.

"Long had I kept the counsel of Daedalus, the great artificer. A stronger opponent of joining our worlds you will not find. But even he could not persuade me any longer. Tonight, with your assistance, I will at long last garner the support needed to convince Lord Zeus himself!" King Alphaios exclaimed.

"Zeus is going to be here tonight?" Maia asked.

"So it has been promised," said King Alphaios, a broad smile spreading across his face. "It is a glorious—"

Maia shuddered as a knock sounded at the doors of the throne room.

"Enter," called King Alphaios, his eyes fixed steely on Maia.

One of the king's young advisors opened the doors and poked his head into the throne room. "Your highness, all of your guests are assembled, and—"

"All of them?" King Alphaios interrupted, raising his head.

"Almost all of them," answered the young man. "Forgive me, your highness, but your guests are quite restless. A few are threatening to take leave if—"

"Who dares suggest leaving?" bellowed King Alphaios. He turned back to Maia. "Perhaps your moment is going to come sooner than I thought, child."

Silently, Maia scolded herself again for taking off the bracelet Icarus gave her.

"Guard!" King Alphaios yelled.

Ophelos pushed past the king's advisor. "Yes, your highness."

"In ten minute's time, you are to bring the girl to the banquet hall. Bring her directly there and do not allow her to speak to anyone else."

King Alphaios walked over to Maia and placed his hand on her shoulder.

"Child, with any luck, you will change this world forever."

With that, the king turned and, ushering his advisor out of the room, left Maia alone with Ophelos. Maia sized the guard up. Something about Ophelos reminded Maia of her physical education teacher, Mr. Dixon, though she doubted he would ever be caught wearing a tunic. Maia walked over to the wall and sat against it.

"You must stand," Ophelos commanded.

"Why?" Maia asked.

"You must stand," the guard repeated.

Groaning, Maia stood and went over to a window. Maia wondered if Mr. Dixon's doppelganger would go after her if she jumped. Beyond the castle walls, Maia could just make out the harbor. Somewhere past the harbor was the way home, she thought. "But I'd need a boat or a winged horse or something else to get there," Maia mumbled.

Behind her, Ophelos gave a low cough.

Maia was beginning to think that she'd imagined her conversation with Icarus in the cell. He would have come by now, Maia reasoned, unless there was something or someone preventing him. She doubted that Icarus would attempt to rescue her during the feast with so many people present. Then again, perhaps she didn't need to be rescued. King Alphaios could be telling the truth, and she would be allowed to return home after the feast. Maia shook her head. When she did get home, she couldn't even begin to think of how to explain any of this to her mother.

Lost in her thoughts, Maia was surprised to see a large flock of birds pass by the window. There was something odd about their formation. She craned her neck to see where the birds were heading and in doing so leaned out the window.

Maia felt a hand grab her and pull her to the floor. She turned to see Ophelos towering over her. "You will stay away from the window!" he snapped.

"You don't have to push me around!" Maia yelled back.

"Stand up," Ophelos ordered.

Maia glared at the guard, not caring if she caused him further anger.

"I said to stand up!"

"You pulled me to the floor," Maia exclaimed. "If you didn't want me down here, you shouldn't have touched me!"

Ophelos stared at her for a moment.

"You were leaning out of the window. You could have fallen. Now, please stand up," Ophelos said, as he held out his hand to help her.

Maia was surprised to hear the change of tone in Ophelos's voice. She stood without taking his hand. As she smoothed out her gown, Maia looked Ophelos in the eye, trying to decide whether to trust him or not.

"How much longer do we have to wait?" Maia asked.

"Just a few more minutes."

Encouraged by Ophelos's air of kindness, Maia took a chance in further gaining his sympathy. "Do you know what's going to happen to me?" Maia asked. "Akantha said I'm going to be sacrificed."

Ophelos grimaced. "I am sure that is not the case. The princess has a tendency to exaggerate."

"There are people here tonight who want me dead. The king told me so. He wants me alive, but some people would like Akantha to be right."

"King Alphaios is a good man. He will protect you," Ophelos assured her.

"But what if he can't? If the gods command him to kill me, what could he do to stop them?"

"There is no point in discussing this any further," Ophelos replied. "We will wait in silence until it is time to leave."

Maia sensed that Ophelos was unsettled with what she'd told him and decided to push a little harder.

"Y-you could help me," Maia stammered. "I need to leave the castle before the feast. Please, I just want to go back home. I want to see my mother."

Though Ophelos said nothing, Maia was sure she was reaching him.

"I don't belong here. I have nothing to do with this place. If you help me leave the castle, I can make it the rest of the way by myself. Please, won't you help me get home to my mother?"

Ophelos walked to the window. He stood in silence for a minute. Maia was about to renew her pleading when he turned and faced her.

"It is time," he said.

CHAPTER 19

THE BANQUET HALL

WITH LITTLE HOPE REMAINING, the castle felt much colder to Maia. She shivered as Ophelos led her from the throne room and down another long hallway. Though he kept his eyes forward, Ophelos seemed to take notice of Maia's uneasiness.

"There is no reason to be nervous," the guard asserted. "You will be protected."

Ophelos's words brought Maia little comfort. She hadn't felt any genuine sense of being protected since throwing away the bracelet.

Maia and Ophelos walked in silence for several minutes. As they turned the last of many corners, Maia heard music and a flood of voices. She realized they were nearing the banquet hall and with it what might prove to be the most important moment of her young life.

As Maia and Ophelos drew closer, the din of the banquet hall throbbed down the hallway in waves. Maia's heart pounded so intensely that she could hear it in her ears. She was startled as a small door flew open, and a boy in a dark gray tunic, no older than Maia, ran straight into Ophelos, nearly dropping the large tray he was carrying.

"Out of the way!" the boy shouted, attempting to push past the guard.

Ophelos reached out and grabbed the boy by his hair, causing him to cry out.

"You will stay out of our way, servant," Ophelos told the unlucky boy, "or the king will have your head."

Whimpering, the servant looked at Ophelos with tears in his eyes. The boy's lip quivered as he took notice of Maia.

"I am s-sorry! I did not know she—"

Grunting, Ophelos released his grip on the servant's hair. Caught off-balance, the boy fell to the ground, scattering the contents of his tray. He scrambled to collect everything he'd dropped.

"What is going on out here?" a familiar voice roared. Maia clenched her teeth as Aeton came toward her and Ophelos.

"This servant threatened to harm the king's guest," Ophelos answered.

"Well, we cannot have that," Aeton said, forcing a grin.

Aeton grabbed Maia by the chin, causing her to wince.

"If any harm is to come to this wretched little creature, it will be at my hand," Aeton continued.

"No harm will come to her!" Ophelos shouted. He knocked Aeton's arm away and, to Maia's great relief, pulled her to his side.

"You dare touch me? I am the king's most valued agent, and you are nothing but—"

"Aeton, that is enough," interrupted Kastor, as he wobbled down the hallway. "The king is already quite angry with you for your behavior on the ship. I suggest you keep your hands off the girl."

Spitting, Aeton turned and walked away. "Move!" he shouted to the servant as the boy collected the last of his goods and ran down the hallway.

"Are you hurt, Maia?" Kastor asked.

Maia shook her head.

"Good," Kastor said. "The king left you in safe hands with Ophelos, but I will take you from here."

Maia looked at Ophelos, but the guard's face showed little expression.

"You may return to your post."

Ophelos bowed his head before marching off, leaving Maia alone with Kastor.

"In a moment, we will enter the banquet hall. I understand the king gave you instructions. You are to truthfully answer any question asked of you. Do you understand?"

Maia knew she had little choice in the matter. She nodded her head.

"Excellent. Everything is going to be fine. Come with me," Kastor directed.

Maia followed Kastor down the hallway. The noise from the banquet hall seemed to grow louder and louder, and Maia was able to make out several distinct voices over the music. Kastor stopped at a pair of large, wooden doors and knocked repeatedly. He waited a few moments and then pounded on the doors again.

With a menacing creak, the doors slowly opened. Kastor took Maia by the arm and waddled into the banquet hall. A few notes of music hung in the air. The loud buzzing of voices was replaced with an eerie whispering. A gaggle of women clad in skimpy robes ran past Kastor and Maia out of the banquet hall. They were followed by four young men carrying a variety of musical instruments Maia had seen in her books on ancient Greece. As she adjusted to the light in the banquet hall, Maia's face went red as dozens of pairs of eyes scrutinized her. It was daunting to make sense of the bizarre scene before her.

Kastor stopped in the center of the banquet hall between two long, wooden tables littered with gold plates and goblets. Sitting at the tables were several men of varying ages with curious looks on their faces. Behind the tables were rows of burning torches that cast flickering light on the marble statues of gods and goddesses lining the walls of the banquet hall. On an altar platform at the head of the room, King Alphaios looked out over the hall from a gilded throne. Maia noticed Aeton standing in a corner, glaring at her. Disturbed by his presence, she turned her attention to the hall's high ceiling, which was capped with a large, glass dome.

"There!" King Alphaios bellowed. "There is the proof of which I spoke."

A muttering came from the men seated at the tables. The expressions on their faces varied from ones of excitement to outright disgust. After some time, one of the men called out, "What proof? It is just a girl!"

"Just a girl?" King Alphaios repeated. "I bring no ordinary girl before you today. This child is of both worlds. She is proof of all that can be attained by the rejoining."

The men resumed their muttering. Maia looked at the king, his face doing little to mask his displeasure at the reception being given to her.

"Kastor, bring the girl here!" King Alphaios commanded.

"Come," Kastor instructed, again taking Maia by the arm. He brought her to the first altar step, where King Alphaios joined her. Kastor bowed before retreating to the corner opposite where Aeton stood watch.

"This child lives in the world so many of you fear," King Alphaios stated, "a world that should no longer be kept out of our reach."

"You are brave now, Alphaios," called out one of the men, "but what would you say if the gods knew of your desire?"

King Alphaios laughed. "What makes you say the gods do not know of what I seek? Is it not possible the gods themselves are conflicted?"

"That is heresy!" called out another of the men. "The gods do not want to see our welfare compromised! They created Olympia to protect us from harm."

"And what harm could come from rejoining our worlds, I ask you," countered King Alphaios. "What dangers might exist? Lord Zeus's sacred emissary, this very girl's father, was willing to forsake our world for the other. How dangerous could it be?"

"We have heard these same arguments before, Alphaios," said an older man of regal bearing in bright cobalt robes seated in the front of the banquet hall. "I am not impressed that you have brought this girl here, regardless of who her father was."

Maia flinched. Once again, her father was spoken of so casually by people she didn't know.

"Send her back home," the man in cobalt continued, "for there is nothing that can alter my judgment. Should the gods call upon us for counsel, I will support keeping our worlds apart."

"Here, here!" called out several of the men. Soon, the banquet hall was brimming with noise as the greater part of those in the audience voiced their disapproval.

"Quiet!" shouted King Alphaios. "You will grant me your attention – now!"

The men at the tables continued to squabble. Maia looked at the king who, ignoring the disquiet in the banquet hall, appeared to be making every effort to remain calm.

"Very soon," King Alphaios said, "you will indeed be called upon to offer your advice. If the gods come to learn that a member of this council, first assembled by Lord Zeus himself, has been as disrespected as I have been, they will be most displeased."

To Maia's surprise, the men quieted and turned their attention back to the king.

"We have been given a sacred trust, and it is our responsibility to see that we do not violate it," the king concluded.

The man in cobalt robes spoke again. "What would you have us do, Alphaios?"

"I would have you, Patrikios, and the other members of this council, take this opportunity to ask the girl any questions you may possess."

Again, all eyes fell upon Maia. She took several short breaths. Just answer honestly, Maia reminded herself, and it will all be over soon.

CHAPTER 20

THE GLASS DOME

"I HAVE A QUESTION," said a man sitting a few feet away from Maia.

Here we go, Maia thought, as she picked at her fingernails.

"Until you journeyed to our world, what did you know of the gods of Olympus?"

What did I know, Maia repeated to herself. Her thoughts wandered back to her many afternoons in the library.

"Answer me!"

Swallowing loudly, Maia replied, "I b-believed that the gods were just part of stories. I didn't think they were real. No one in my world still believes that the gods of Olympus exist."

The men grumbled, several of them openly arguing the merits of Maia's response.

"See, it is as we were told!" called out a man seated in the back of the banquet hall. "They have forsaken our gods."

"That is enough!" warned King Alphaios. "Ask another question."

Maia's eyes darted around the hall as she waited for someone else to speak. Several moments passed before a man seated in front of Maia finally asked, "Alphaios, what would you have us inquire of her? She is but a child. Can we expect her to tell us how the leaders of her world would respond to the return of the gods? What could she know of such things?"

Again, the men began to argue amongst themselves. With a scowl, King Alphaios raised his arms as he prepared to chastise them once more.

"I don't think they'd like it," Maia offered, her voice rising above the angry exchanges being had between the men.

King Alphaios himself showed surprise that Maia had answered the half-posed question.

"And why is that, child?" the king asked.

Maia clenched her hands as she answered. "Because from everything I've read, the gods always made a mess of the lives of regular people. They thought they were making things better, but they were really just making things worse. I don't think the leaders of my world would like that."

"Do you trust your leaders?" asked the man in front.

"Some of them," Maia answered, her voice growing steadier, "but I guess they make mistakes like the gods did too."

"You hold the opinion that the gods are capable of making mistakes?" asked the man called Patrikios.

"But that's why you're all here," Maia answered, finally unclenching her hands. "Didn't the gods create this place because they made too many mistakes back in my world?" Maia paused. "If the two worlds were brought back together, how do you know they wouldn't make the same mistakes all over again?"

The men were silent – even the king said nothing. Maia was afraid she'd gone too far. She bowed her head, preparing to be punished for her words.

"She is quite brave, Alphaios," said Patrikios, breaking the long silence. "This child may have more value than I thought."

"Would you agree then, my brothers, that this matter warrants further debate?" asked the king.

Maia raised her head. A few of the men gave each other cautious glances, but none spoke. In the corner of the room, Maia could see Aeton snickering. She looked to Kastor, who nodded his head approvingly at her.

"Well then," King Alphaios asked, "does no one wish to speak?"

Before any of the men could answer the king, the walls of the banquet hall began to shake. Maia searched for something against which to brace herself. The light from the torches flickered wildly, making the statues of the gods and goddesses appear to sway. A few of the men got to their feet. Maia watched Kastor for a sign of what to do, but he appeared as ill as he'd been on the wagon they rode up from the harbor.

After several seconds, the shaking subsided, and as it did a bright, golden light filled the glass dome above the hall, casting the entire room in its powerful glow. Maia shielded her eyes, trying not to stumble over anything as she backed away from the altar.

A voice not unlike thunder echoed throughout the banquet hall. "Your lord and master will speak!"

Maia watched in surprise as the men, including the king, dropped to their knees.

"Lord Zeus!" cried King Alphaios. "You honor us!"

"And you dishonor Lord Zeus with this gathering, Alphaios," boomed the voice of Zeus, king of the gods. "To what end did you bring this child here?"

"Lord Zeus, I meant no dishonor," King Alphaios said. "We who are trusted with the knowledge of the sacred origins of our world sought only to better understand why—"

"There is nothing for you to understand," Zeus thundered. "You overestimate your importance. You and the others are merely to serve at the pleasure of the gods of Olympus. Was your duty not made clear?"

"My lord, please, I do wish to serve you. But... but there are those of us who have our doubts."

Maia cringed. Based on everything that she'd read about Zeus's foul temper, she was certain that King Alphaios was about to be struck down by a bolt of lightning. Continuing to shield her eyes, Maia waited anxiously for it to come.

Instead of lightning, it was Zeus's thunderous voice that filled the hall. "So be it, Alphaios. If you choose to doubt your lord and master, then you are a lost man, without the protection of the gods. There are others more worthy, and it is they who shall be honored to keep the counsel of Lord Zeus."

As his last words echoed throughout the banquet hall, the bright light faded from the glass dome. Maia stood unsteadily just beneath it, expecting yet more of Zeus's wrath.

For a moment, all was quiet – until a voice abounding with terror filled the still shuddering banquet hall. "No!" King Alphaios called out. "My lord, do not forsake me!"

Maia looked at her host. The king, who only moments before was so certain of his triumph, lay crumpled on the floor sobbing. The other men remained kneeling, speechless after their brief audience with Lord Zeus. The king's cries were all that could be heard.

After several minutes, the older man called Patrikios stood, straightened his robes, and approached the fallen king.

"You have jeopardized us all today, Alphaios," Patrikios said, his voice revealing no trace of pity. He turned and exited through the doors of the hall. The other men followed without a sound, leaving the banquet hall empty except for Kastor, Aeton, Maia, and the king.

It was Kastor who was the first to speak. "Your highness, what can I do?" he asked.

King Alphaios raised his head. He looked across the banquet hall, his eyes red and narrowed, before settling upon Maia. The king's expression startled her.

"You can get this useless girl out of my sight," King Alphaios said, striking the floor with his fist. The king stood and brushed past Maia and Kastor.

"With pleasure, your highness," answered Aeton, as the king exited the hall, "with pleasure."

Aeton crept over to Maia, his eyes like that of a lion about to pounce its prey.

"Now, Aeton, do not do anything rash!" Kastor pleaded. "The king is distressed, but he would not want any harm to—"

"That is enough from you, Kastor." Aeton drew a small knife from his belt. Before Kastor realized what his comrade was about to do, Aeton brought the handle of the knife down hard on Kastor's head, knocking him out.

"Now, girl, there is no one left to protect you... not even a mouse," Aeton said, as he juggled the knife from hand to hand.

Maia backed away, but Aeton quickly grabbed her. As he pulled Maia in – so close that she could feel his warm, sticky breath – the banquet hall was suddenly filled with the explosive sound of shattering glass from above as a large, winged figure crashed through the dome, landing atop Aeton. Just managing to escape being cut by the falling glass, Maia stumbled, falling onto her back. The winged figure raised its head.

"Icarus?"

"Come, Maia," Icarus answered. "It is time to take you home."

CHAPTER 21

ESCAPE THE CASTLE

"ICARUS, HOW ON EARTH did you do that?" Maia asked, looking at the shattered dome above them.

Icarus smirked. "We are not *on* earth."

Aeton groaned as he attempted to lift himself up. Icarus pulled a club from his belt and gave Aeton an unceremonious thump on his head.

"I wish you'd let me do that," Maia said.

"Gods willing, you will have another opportunity to exact your revenge on Aeton for his cruelty, but for now my blow will have to suffice. We have little time, Maia."

Icarus stood, allowing Maia to fully take in the large, white-feathered wings strapped to his arms and back.

"Where did you get those?" Maia asked.

"From my father, of course. There is almost nothing that my father cannot—"

"Yeah, yeah, I know. He's the greatest," Maia teased.

"For someone who has endured as much as you have, you are in surprisingly good spirits," Icarus said, raising his eyebrows.

Maia felt her face go pink. "Um, shouldn't we get going?"

"Yes, this way," Icarus said, directing her toward the king's throne. "There is an exit behind here."

"How do you know?"

"There are many things about this castle to which I am privy," Icarus said.

"Oh, yeah. I forgot you and the princess go way back," Maia retorted.

"Akantha spoke of me, did she?"

"She spoke of you, alright."

Icarus ran his hands over several large stones in the wall behind the king's throne, not seeming to take notice of Maia's distaste for the princess.

"Here it is," Icarus said. As he pushed against one of the larger stones, the wall gave way to an opening. "This will lead us to a passage out of the castle."

Icarus stepped into the opening. Before following him, Maia looked up at the dome. Beyond the shards of glass, the sky was a tapestry of heavenly bodies. Night had fallen.

"Maia, come."

Maia joined Icarus in the opening behind the throne. As Icarus pushed the wall back into place, she heard Aeton let out a moan.

"I hope he's in a lot of pain."

"Maia, please forget about Aeton for now. Follow me," directed Icarus.

"How can I follow you if I can't see you?" asked Maia. Without the opening, there was no source of light.

"Take my hand," answered Icarus.

"What? Oh, okay," Maia said, as she wiped her hand on the front of her gown.

Maia reached out and took Icarus's hand. He gave hers a light squeeze, and Maia nearly pulled away.

"I am sorry about the wax on my fingers. It is what keeps the feathers in place."

"Oh... uh... it's fine," Maia said. "Can we just get out of here?"

"Of course," Icarus replied. "Do not worry, Maia. I will lead you to safety."

Slowly, they made their way through the hidden passage. Maia stumbled occasionally, but, despite the darkness and the urgency of their task, she felt unexpectedly confident being led by Icarus. Rounding a corner, they paused in a section of the passage where light came in from an opening near the top. Maia found herself staring at Icarus who, she was relieved to see, was too distracted to notice.

Icarus motioned for Maia to remain quiet. As they inched their way down the passage, they heard a voice – a rather loud and familiar one, in fact – come from the opening.

"It is not fair!"

"It never is with her," Icarus whispered.

Maia stifled a laugh.

"Why do I never get what I want?" Akantha continued to shout on the other side of the wall.

Something fairly large hit the wall with a crash. Rather than wait to hear the rest of Akantha's tantrum, Icarus and Maia continued down the passage. As they plunged back into darkness, Icarus let out a breath.

"Gods, I do not miss that," he whispered, shaking his head. Maia allowed herself a small smile.

After ten minutes or so, having made many turns and descended several sets of steps, Icarus came to a stop.

"We will wait here."

"For what?" Maia asked. "Shouldn't we keep moving?"

Icarus let go of Maia's hand, and she felt his wings brush her side. He was running his hands along the wall. Maia also reached out and pressed the cold, damp stones in front of her.

A loud knock came from the other side of the wall, startling Maia. She grabbed Icarus by the arm.

"That is the signal, Maia. I will need your help."

Icarus took Maia's hands and placed them on the wall, laying his own hands beside hers.

"Please, help me push." With some effort on their part, the wall at last gave way to an opening. Feeling the cool rush of night air, Maia nearly squealed with joy at having managed to escape the castle. Her excitement was short-lived as she found herself face to face with Ophelos, the guard who earlier had ignored her pleas for help.

"No!" Maia cried. "Icarus, it's a trap!"

"Maia, do not panic," Icarus said, putting his hand on her shoulder. "Ophelos is here to help us."

"Him? Help us?"

"Quiet!" Ophelos commanded. "If you keep making so much noise, we will be discovered."

Maia resisted accepting Icarus's claim. "If he's here to help, then why didn't he set me free earlier?"

"We had to follow the plan, Maia," Icarus explained. "Certain events had to play out before you could be rescued."

Maia looked at Ophelos's eyes for some trace of the compassion she'd sensed earlier that would allow her to trust him now.

Noting Maia's lasting suspicion, Icarus added, "Ophelos has been working with my father for a very long time. There is no need to worry."

"Both of you need to lower your voices," Ophelos scolded.

"Does the king know the castle was breached?" Icarus asked.

"Of course the king knows. You destroyed his banquet hall," said Ophelos irritably. "Icarus, you were supposed to go in through a window."

Icarus's face turned a deep scarlet. "I thought crashing through the dome would be, um, more—"

"Impressive?" Ophelos suggested.

"It is done, Ophelos," Icarus said, glancing sideways at Maia.

"Yes, except that the grounds are now crawling with guards. You will have to hide in the woods until a distraction can be created."

"But I thought there were dangerous creatures in the woods," Maia said tensely.

"There is nothing so frightening in the woods that I cannot handle, Maia," Icarus boasted.

Ignoring him, Maia asked Ophelos, "Is it safe?"

"But I—"

"There is no other choice, and it will be for just a short while," Ophelos interrupted. "I have to convince the other guards that you were taken in the direction of the harbor."

"But aren't we going to the harbor?" Maia asked, looking back and forth between Icarus and Ophelos. "How else are we going to get off the island?"

Icarus gave Maia a broad smile.

"Have you ever wondered what it would be like to fly?"

CHAPTER 22

DEEPER INTO THE WOODS

MAIA REMEMBERED THE FIRST TIME her mother yelled at her for rolling her eyes. She'd just picked Maia up from school and was thrilled by the news that third-grade students were allowed to start playing a musical instrument. They were a few blocks away from school, and her mother had already mentioned twice that Maia could possibly receive a music scholarship to college when she saw Maia roll her eyes in the car's rearview mirror. While the rest of the ride was unpleasant for both of them, it was hardly the last time Maia had been caught engaging in that particular act.

"Maia, is there something wrong with your eyes?" asked Icarus.

"No, but there must be something wrong with my ears. Am I supposed to climb on your back and let you carry me to the mainland?"

Icarus laughed. "No, of course not. These wings could never support both of us."

Maia heaved a sigh of relief.

"There is another pair of wings for you!" said Icarus, nearly bursting with excitement.

"Are you insane?" Maia shouted.

"Quiet!" Ophelos told them. "There is no time for bickering. We must get you to the woods – now!"

Still thinking about Icarus's troubling idea of an escape plan, Maia followed the guard and her doggedly frustrating rescuer across the wide expanse of the king's gardens. As they approached the woods, Maia recalled the sense she had earlier of something watching her. The woods were the last place Maia wanted to hide, but what choice did she have? Once again, she was made to put her faith in others. Even if Ophelos proved trustworthy, Maia still wasn't sure what to make of Icarus.

Ophelos and Icarus ran straight into the woods with Maia right behind them. They stopped running after a few minutes under the cover of the trees. The woods were dark – nearly as dark as the passage she and Icarus had taken out of the castle. This time, however, Maia had little inclination to hold Icarus's hand.

Ophelos motioned to Maia to crouch behind a large, fallen tree. She complied, and Icarus joined her.

"You will wait here until I return," Ophelos instructed. "With any luck, I will only be gone a short while."

Ophelos stood and pulled his sword from its sheath on his belt.

"Do not do anything foolish," he called, knocking away a low-hanging branch with his sword.

"I will make sure she does not," Icarus called back.

Maia thought she heard Ophelos mutter, "Lord Zeus, give me strength," as he vanished from sight.

Alone with Icarus, Maia tried her best to remain calm. So far, there didn't appear to be anything dangerous nearby, and the only sound was coming from Icarus, as he had to adjust his position several times before he could sit comfortably.

"You're making too much noise," Maia warned.

"I am sorry. These wings can be difficult to shift."

"And you want me to wear a pair of those too? Why didn't you just bring Pierinos?"

"Pierinos escaped again. Though it was not my fault, Father blames me," said Icarus with apparent shame.

"So, he's punishing you by making you wear those?" Maia asked, pointing at the wings.

"It is not a punishment, Maia. My father's faith in me was restored after I rescued you on the Acropolis. Still, he could not risk sending me with another of Lord Zeus's precious winged stallions. The wings he invented are a suitable alternative."

"You flew all the way here?"

"Yes, and as soon as Ophelos returns we will retrieve the other pair of wings from their hiding place behind the king's stables, and you and I will fly away from this island."

"Why don't you just shoot an arrow at me again or use one of those flashbulb things? I'd be home in seconds. You could've even done it back in the cell."

"I cannot bring you back to your world while we are on this island. It does not exist there."

"But you said everything was physically the same in the two worlds."

"There are some exceptions. The gods created this island for King Alphaios, which is also why we must leave as soon as possible. With the king having lost the favor of Lord Zeus, there is no telling how much longer before the island is destroyed. Lord Zeus has quite a temper."

Maia thought carefully about how to ask her next question, not wanting to sound arrogant or to offend the boy who'd just rescued her.

"Icarus, there's something I still don't understand. If I'm as important as everyone keeps saying, why didn't your father come himself? What else was so vital for him to deal with that he sent you?"

Maia was relieved to see that Icarus didn't appear offended in the least. He did, however, give her a very grave look and nearly whisper as he answered her question.

"Even if Father was not elsewhere dealing with the fallout of your abduction, he could not have come. He and King Alphaios were once the closest of confidants, but a great rift formed between them. The king made it very clear that Father should never return here. He would be captured and put to death."

"But what about you? Why wouldn't the king put you to death?" Maia asked, revealing more concern for Icarus than she cared to make known.

"Ah, I thought you said Akantha spoke of me. If she did, it should be clear that the princess would never allow me to be harmed in any way."

"So, you two are an item?"

"A what?"

"An item. A couple. You and the princess?"

Icarus began to laugh, but caught himself before he made too much noise.

"No, Maia. As much as Akantha would like to think that I am going to rescue her from her poor, overindulged life, I am not. Please do not think less of me, but I used her affection as a means of getting better acquainted with her father's castle."

"Why? What's so important about the castle?"

"Though his status has greatly diminished after what occurred tonight, King Alphaios long held a position of favor with the gods. Father suspected that there were great riches – and I do not refer to gold and jewels – hidden within the castle's walls. During his meetings with the king, Akantha was quite happy to show me every secret the castle afforded, which was certainly to our advantage tonight."

Maia had to agree with Icarus. She also had to admit she was glad that Icarus also held Akantha in little regard, even though she didn't like that it mattered to her.

"Did you enjoy your time with the princess?" Icarus asked.

"What do you think?"

"I do not know. I would not profess to know or understand the workings of a girl's mind," Icarus answered, blushing.

"You know, you really are infuriating sometimes."

"Only sometimes?"

Maia smirked. "Don't push your luck."

"You are not like other girls, Maia. You are nothing like the princess."

"That's good to hear at least."

"Perhaps it is fortunate you never knew of your importance here."

"There's a big part of me that wishes I still didn't know," Maia stated.

Icarus opened his mouth to speak, but no words of comfort would come. Instead, he gave Maia a gentle nod.

"So... we wait?" Maia asked.

"Yes, we wait."

* * *

THOUGH OPHELOS HAD STATED his intention to return in a short while, this didn't come to pass. Minutes stretched into hours, and, while there were several times when it sounded as though someone was approaching, the guard didn't return. Despite her uneasiness, Maia found her eyes closing. As she drifted off to sleep, several images crossed her mind, including that of the sea god Triton rising from the harbor in Sea Cliff.

"He was watching me," Maia said dreamily. "The gods have been watching me."

Maia awoke with a start.

"Icarus, wake up!" she cried.

"Maia, what is it? Why are you making so much noise?" asked Icarus, who'd also fallen asleep.

"We have to go!" Maia exclaimed, jumping to her feet. "We have to go now!"

"We cannot leave, Maia. We must wait for Ophelos. He will return soon."

"Icarus, look at the sky. It's almost morning. Ophelos has been gone for hours. He's not coming back. Something must've happened to him."

Icarus gazed up through the trees. The sky was beginning to lighten.

"Eos is preparing to open the gates of sunrise."

A few weeks ago, Maia would have found such a comment ridiculous, but after everything she'd experienced during her time in Greece she simply nodded in agreement.

"Yeah, sure. But we need to move. Icarus, the gods won't let any harm come to me. They've been watching over me, protecting me, ever since this whole mess started. You said yourself that they answered my cry for help back in the cell. Divine intervention, right? Even without Ophelos, we'll be fine."

Icarus rubbed his chin. "Maia, if you are wrong—"

"We can't stay here forever. If we go now, there'll still be enough darkness to cover us. How do we get to the stables from here?"

Icarus scrunched up his face. When he spoke, there was still more than a hint of uncertainty in his voice.

"We go in that direction," he said, pointing. "The quickest way will be to go deeper into the woods before we exit near the stables."

Maia took several deep breaths. "The gods will protect me," she repeated softly. Maia envisioned herself back in Sea Cliff, sitting on her bench overlooking the harbor. The gods would see her there again. She just needed to have faith.

"Fine," Maia said, "let's go."

CHAPTER 23

THE SHEER WONDER OF FLYING

ICARUS AND MAIA started their trek deeper into the woods.

"We will have to hurry, Maia. Stay close, for I do not know what we might encounter."

Overhead, the sky was streaked with the early light of sunrise. "The gods will protect me," Maia repeated.

"What did you say?"

"Nothing. It's getting brighter out."

"At least we will be able to better see where we are going," offered Icarus, sensing Maia's worry. "I have been in these woods many times. I will get us out safely."

"The gods will protect me," Maia said again, the words taking on a rhythm. She desperately hoped the gods were indeed watching over her, as her resolve was tested with the crackling of each footstep. The farther she and Icarus ventured into the woods, the more the trees seemed to pulsate with danger.

Icarus came to an abrupt stop.

"Maia, do not move," Icarus whispered. "There is something up ahead."

Maia crouched close to the ground, her heart pounding.

"What is it?" she whispered back.

Icarus took several seconds to respond. "It... yes, it is gone, Maia. We can move on."

Maia was about to get to her feet when an odd shadow crossed her face. She opened her mouth to scream a warning, but it was too late. A creature with the body of a lion and the head and wings of an eagle had leapt out from the stand of trees behind Maia and knocked Icarus face forward to the ground.

Maia shrieked as the ferocious creature clawed at the wings on Icarus's back. Alerted to her presence, it raised its head and narrowed its eyes at Maia. The creature turned away from Icarus and, letting out a deafening roar, began to circle her. Maia searched the ground for something to use to defend herself but found nothing other than a few short branches.

"The gods will protect me. The gods will protect me," Maia repeated in a desperate whisper.

The creature and Maia locked eyes just as it pounced. Maia dropped to the ground and squeezed her eyes shut, steeling herself for the attack. But instead of the feeling she'd anticipated of the creature's claws carving into her, Maia opened her eyes to the sickening sound of metal piercing flesh. The creature, which lay moaning before her, had been felled by a sword. Maia drew back in surprise as she spotted the swordsman jump down from a ridge behind her. Ophelos pulled his sword from the creature's side and plunged it back into its neck, silencing the frightful beast.

"Ophelos!" Maia cried out in relief.

The guard didn't appear nearly as happy to see Maia as she was to see him.

"Why did you move?" he asked, as he pulled Maia to her feet.

"We didn't think you were coming back. I thought we'd be safe as long as... "

Maia was relieved to not have to explain herself further, seeing as Ophelos had turned his attention to Icarus as he stirred on the ground surrounded by feathers.

"Icarus, are you hurt?"

"I do not think so," Icarus answered, as he examined the damage to his wings. "I am sorry, Ophelos. We should not have left without you."

"It took longer than I thought. King Alphaios himself is commanding the search."

"We must get to the stables."

"This way," the guard said, indicating the direction with his bloodied sword. With Ophelos leading, they reached the edge of the woods in short order. Able to see a larger expanse of the sky, Maia cringed as she realized how exposed they would be once they left the cover of the trees.

"There!" Icarus exclaimed. "There are the king's stables, behind which are hidden your wings."

"Wait," Maia said, recognizing that they were short one pair of wings. She turned to Ophelos. "What about you?"

"You need not worry about me, Maia. No one knows of my role in tonight's events. After I see you safely off the island, I will rejoin the guards in your pursuit."

"Please, we must go – now!" Icarus insisted.

Ophelos parted the remaining branches separating them from the grassy area that would lead, if Icarus could be trusted, to the stables – and at last to freedom.

"Are we going to make a run for it?" Maia asked in a whisper.

"If the gods allow," Ophelos replied. "Wait! Get behind me!"

"What is it?" asked Icarus.

"Two of the king's guards. But they appear to be leaving."

Sitting on a branch high above them, a bird chirped, ready for the new day. The sound filled Maia with unexpected dread. So much could still go wrong. What if the wings didn't work?

"They are gone. We go now!" Ophelos commanded.

As they made their way to the stables, Maia noticed that Icarus was leaving a trail of feathers in his wake.

"Hurry," called Ophelos.

"Praise you, Ophelos," cried Icarus, turning to the horizon, "for this will be a glorious day indeed."

"Do not praise me, Icarus, for I have led us into a trap. Take cover!"

A guard stood behind the stables, a bow and arrow in hand. Maia flashed to the day she first met Icarus and how it was an arrow that first brought her to this unexpected adventure. As the guard let the arrow fly, Maia felt oddly calm, as if this was in some way how her journey was meant to end.

But before such an ending could play out, Ophelos gave a mighty cry and dove into the path of the arrow. It hit him squarely in the chest.

"No!" Maia shouted, as she saw Ophelos struck down. Another arrow flew, this time hitting Icarus in one of his wings, pinning him to the ground.

The guard ran from the stables, pulling a sword from his belt. "Your sacrifice is in vain, traitor," the guard spat at Ophelos. "The girl will die, and you will watch."

The guard raised his sword and, for what seemed to be the third or fourth time in as many hours, Maia braced herself for what might be her final breath. Instead, it was the guard who gasped for air as Ophelos drove his sword, the blood on it barely dry from its last kill, into the guard's back.

"You are a poor archer. And an even poorer swordsman," Ophelos declared in a weakened voice.

The guard fell to the ground, silent.

"Ophelos, how?"

"What manner of guard would I be if I did not protect my charge?" Ophelos whispered before closing his eyes for the last time.

"Ophelos!" Maia said, shaking his arm. "Ophelos, no!"

From behind her, Icarus said, "Maia, please, I need your help."

"He's dead. Ophelos is dead."

"Then we must make certain that he died for a just cause. Help me pull this arrow out."

Maia gave Ophelos one last look. "Thank you," she said softly.

"Maia, please, we do not have much time."

"Are you hurt?"

"Only my pride, something to which I am quite accustomed. The arrow missed my arm, but I cannot free my wing. You must pull it out."

With some effort, Maia was able to free Icarus. In doing so, she tumbled backward, nearly landing atop the dead guard who'd fired the arrows.

"Thank you." Icarus stood and surveyed the bodies. "Ophelos was an honorable man."

Maia got to her feet. "Icarus – the stables."

"Of course. I will show you where the wings are hidden."

Once behind the stables, Icarus pulled at several long, thin planks of wood, behind which lay a pair of wings.

"Here, let me help you."

As Icarus fastened the wings to her back, Maia was struck by the enormity of the night's events. Blood had been shed over her and, if what she'd been told about a war was true, there was more to come.

"There. You are ready."

Icarus flashed his familiar foolish grin, and Maia grudgingly smiled in return.

"Maia, I—"

"What?"

"I just want you to know that... well, what I am trying to say is—"

"How could you bring her here?" asked an icy voice from the shadows.

They weren't alone. Maia recoiled at the sight of Akantha standing several feet away, caressing a short blade with her fingers. Makeup ran down her face. Akantha's hair was a mess but not nearly as wild as the look in her eyes.

"This was our special place, Icarus, yours and mine. And now you have ruined it!"

"There is nothing special about this place, just as there is nothing special between us."

Akantha waved the blade about. "Why? Why would you choose her over me? I am a princess!"

"Look around you, Akantha. Your father's days as keeper of this kingdom are numbered, as are yours as a princess. The gods favor your father no more."

"No! You are wrong!"

"Akantha, put down that knife. You will hurt yourself, and there has been enough bloodshed this night."

"The only place I will put this blade is in your throat," said Akantha, as she charged Icarus.

Taking advantage of Akantha's blind rage, Maia grabbed a thin, wooden plank that was leaning against the stables. As Akantha passed her, Maia swung the plank like a lacrosse stick, checking Akantha in the stomach. Akantha crashed to the ground, sending the blade flying out of her reach.

Maia ripped off her headpiece and threw it at Akantha. "You can have this back. You're going to need to hold onto as many of your jewels as you can."

Icarus nodded his head. "I am impressed."

Akantha let out a loud sob. Maia strained not to hit her again.

"Maia, we must go. There is a cliff just beyond the stables. From there we will take flight." Leaving the whimpering princess behind, Icarus broke into a run with Maia right behind him.

"You must do as I say," Icarus called to Maia. "The cliff is just up ahead. When I tell you to do so, you must spread your wings."

"And do what?"

"Fly, Maia! You will fly!"

Icarus and Maia ran up a short hill and, as they reached the top, Icarus shouted, "Now!"

Maia raised her arms, spreading her wings. A moment later, the ground disappeared beneath her and to her astonishment Maia took flight.

"Maia, look forward and slowly raise and lower your arms. That is how you will stay aloft."

Maia did as she was told, and, as though flying came as natural as chasing after a lacrosse ball, she soared through the sky, the wind rushing past her and the smell of the sea flooding her nostrils. It was more fantastic than Maia could ever have imagined – even having ridden Pierinos. As she struggled to take in the sheer wonder of flying, Maia had to remind herself to breathe.

"Make certain to keep looking forward," Icarus called, his voice muffled by the wind.

Maia followed Icarus as they flew farther and farther away from King Alphaios's island kingdom. Maia wanted to turn around to look back, but heeded Icarus's instructions. As skeptical as she'd been when he first told her of his plan, Maia was elated that Icarus had come through for her in the end.

"Icarus, this is incredible!"

"Yes, my father is capable of many wonderful things. His son, however, is a fool."

"You're not a fool, Icarus. Why would you say that?" Maia called back.

But in the light of the rising sun, Maia could see that Icarus was fighting to keep his wings moving steadily. Feathers were falling out in large bunches. Maia raised and lowered her wings more quickly and caught up to Icarus.

"The gryphon that attacked us in the woods caused damage far worse than I thought. I cannot continue."

"What do you mean you can't continue, Icarus? What other choice is there?"

"Maia, I am sorry for all of the trouble I have caused you. That was never my intention. I simply thought you should know the truth."

"Icarus, you don't need to apologize. Please, stay with me!"

"Soon you will reach land. You must not fly too close to the sun, nor too close to the sea. But do not fear, Maia. The gods will protect you."

Icarus turned to Maia and feigned a smile. He appeared to linger momentarily before taking a terrifying plunge into the sea below.

Maia looked to the water, but saw no sign of Icarus. He was gone. A strong wind suddenly rose up from the sea jostling Maia. For a moment, she assumed she would meet the same fate as Icarus, but Maia quickly pushed such thoughts away as she righted herself and carried on flapping her wings.

"No!" Maia cried out, blinking back tears. "I've come too far and too many people have made sacrifices for me to give up now. I have to get home."

Maia continued flying for several minutes, roused by the promise of being reunited with her mother. But as the sun rose higher over the horizon, she started to tire. Beads of sweat ran down her brow into her eyes. Her neck and shoulders ached. Despite her strength of spirit, it became more and more difficult to keep her arms moving with enough rhythm to remain steadily airborne. Maia refused to look at the sea, knowing to do so could mark her defeat. Still, in short time even her best efforts couldn't prevent Maia from losing momentum.

"Come on, you can do this. Don't give up now," Maia pleaded.

Maia flapped her arms for another minute or two, desperate to see her escape through to the end. She tried to cry for help, but no longer had the energy to draw enough breath to make a sound. Beyond the point of exhaustion, Maia finally stopped flapping. She looked down at the sea, prepared for it to consume her as it had Icarus.

A few seconds passed, but Maia didn't fall. Instead, she found herself floating in air, surrounded by a warm, golden light. "The gods will protect me," Maia said a final time, her relief at the recurrence of divine intervention tinged with more than its share of fear.

CHAPTER 24

THE SORROW OF LOSS

"YOU HAVE TRAVELED quite far, little one," boomed a voice Maia recognized as that of Zeus, king of the gods.

Though it took Maia a moment to become accustomed to simply floating in the sky, she was relieved to be able to stop flapping her wings. The golden light that surrounded her made it difficult to tell from where the voice of Zeus was coming. Like the light, it seemed to envelop her.

"You are tired," the god continued. "Be assured that your adventure is at an end. You will be returned home safely."

For the first time in days, Maia felt at ease. It was an almost forgotten sensation, especially in Olympia. Even though she was suspended in mid-air, hundreds of feet above the sea, and in the presence of the supreme Greek god, Maia allowed herself to breathe freely.

"You no longer have need of these."

A powerful wind blew, and Maia's wings were ripped from her body. She stretched her arms, which throbbed from the strenuous effort that had kept her aloft.

"You have shown great bravery, child. Your father would be proud."

"You knew my father?"

"She speaks!" The god said with a laugh. "Lord Zeus thought perhaps your trials had rendered you mute."

Maia's face reddened. "I can speak. It's just... well, I've never spoken to a god before."

"Child, there would appear to be many things you have done whilst in Olympia that you have not done before, flying being the least of them."

"Oh, I almost forgot! Icarus fell! His wings were damaged, and he fell into the water."

"This is not the first time the artificer's son has taken a plunge into the sea, nor will it be the last. Actions have a way of repeating themselves in Olympia."

"I don't understand."

"Nor are you meant to. Now, let us set about returning you home."

"Wait, please! There are some things I need to know."

"Do you expect the king of the gods to serve as a storyteller?" Zeus boomed.

Ignoring the god's threatening tone, Maia pressed on. "No, of course not, but you mentioned my father. Please, the only thing I know about him is that he sacrificed his life for this world. But I don't understand why."

"It was his sworn duty. If he did not oblige, this world faced destruction. The repercussions would have been felt in your world as well, and he would have risked your life and the life of your mother."

"But he hurt us anyway. My mother thinks he abandoned us without reason." Maia paused. "She's been hurting... for a very long time."

"It pained your father as much to leave her. Your mother's suffering will ease, child. If there is anything Lord Zeus will promise, it is that."

"Thank you."

"Child, the history of Olympia is marked with pain and sacrifice. Many centuries ago, at the end of another pointless war, the gods of Olympus were dying. Those most responsible gave their existence to create this world so that those who remained might continue to thrive. Hera, wife of Lord Zeus, was amongst those who perished. You are not alone in knowing the sorrow of loss."

While Maia tried to make sense of this revelation, she was more surprised by Zeus's tone. He certainly didn't sound as volatile as he did in the myths she'd read. Where was his legendary temper?

"Icarus said my father's family is from Olympia."

"There is some truth to that."

"And my father, he—"

"Child, the existence of this world rests firmly on his shoulders. You do not need to know more than that," Zeus roared, his voice thundering across the sky.

Maia shuddered. There was the temper she'd expected. Maia wanted to ask more of the king of the gods, but she was afraid of angering Zeus. Also, she realized, Maia dreaded the anguish any new information about her father might cause her.

"Now the time has come for you to return home."

The golden light shimmered, and Maia felt herself moving forward, slowly at first, and then accelerating. After a while, the forward motion stopped, and Maia began to descend. The golden light softened, and Maia felt her feet touch the ground. Before her stood the Temple of Poseidon in perfect form. The light vanished and she heard the god's booming voice once more.

"You will be safe here. Lord Zeus will leave you. Farewell."

"Lord Zeus, wait!" Maia cried.

"What do you want now, child?"

"What if it happens again? What if someone else tries to bring me here?"

"Then they will be defying the wishes of the king of the gods, and they will suffer for their actions," Zeus's voice thundered, shaking the very ground on which Maia stood.

Maia flinched – not from the god's rage but from the thought of going through this all over again.

"Still," Zeus continued, "should you care to return... "

A golden bracelet materialized on Maia's wrist.

"You will be safe from recognition," Zeus continued, "if you wear this bracelet. And as long as you choose to keep your identity secret."

"Why would I want to return?" Maia asked.

"Such boldness!" Zeus laughed, shaking the ground once more. "Because of the wonder of this world and because it is in part your home after all."

"What about the war that's supposed to happen?"

"Child, as long as the gods exist, so shall the possibility of war. Some of the family of Lord Zeus did not learn from their mistakes. Alas, they did not learn from the lessons that led to the creation of this world. But be not afraid. You will be safe. Your father's sacrifice was enough. Should you return, you can do so without fear. So decrees Lord Zeus."

The god spoke no further, and soon Maia knew she was alone. She studied the bracelet, twisting it around her wrist over and over again. A series of symbols circled the outside. Maia couldn't make out their meaning, but she had a sense that the images were of significance to her and, perhaps, to her father. Maia stretched out her arm. The bracelet was thicker, weightier than the one given to her by Icarus.

Maia allowed herself to think of Icarus again. Even with all of the trouble the artificer's son, as Zeus called him, had caused, Maia missed his smile. The history of Olympia was marked with pain and sacrifice, Zeus had said. Standing in front of a temple where many sacrifices had traditionally been made, Maia decided she'd already known enough pain for someone her age.

"Thank the gods you are safe," said a recognizable voice from behind her.

Maia was loath to turn around. She closed her eyes and tried to remember how it felt to fly, but an uncomfortably familiar feeling of betrayal was building inside her, blocking out any possibility of joy.

"You lied to me," Maia said before turning around.

"I had little choice," answered Uncle Dorian. He was wearing a tunic and sandals. The tunic was tattered and had several dark stains.

"My grandfather says we always have choices."

"He sounds very wise."

"Yeah, except he was the one who inspired my mother to let me come to Greece, so I should probably rethink a lot of things he says."

"Maia, please—"

"You realize I could've been killed, right? I was tied up, beaten, forced to put on a pair of wings to escape from an island full of monsters and... "

Maia waved a fist at her uncle.

"And worst yet, I had to spend a whole day playing dress-up with a spoiled princess who makes some girls I know back home look like little angels."

"You have not lost your sense of humor," said Uncle Dorian, a wry smile forming on his lips.

"There's nothing funny about this!" Maia insisted. "Why didn't you tell me the truth? Why did you let me take off the bracelet Icarus gave me?"

The smile faded from Uncle Dorian's face. He opened his mouth to speak, but appeared to change his mind about what he was going to say. After a few moments of thought, he simply offered, "I am sorry."

Maia shook her head. She turned and faced the temple with her back to Uncle Dorian. An apology, though welcome, wasn't what she'd wanted. As Maia watched the colors of the temple's columns change in the light of the rising sun, her anger slowly diminished. What purpose did being angry serve?

Maia stared at the temple. It was beautiful, and its position on a cliff overlooking the sea reminded her of home. If she recalled correctly, it was Friday, and she was due to travel home the next day.

Maia faced her uncle. Seeing again the poor state of his clothing, questions exploded in her head like fireworks. Still, none mattered except for one.

"Can we go home now?"

CHAPTER 25

EVERYTHING THAT MATTERED

A SWIFT WIND WHISTLED through the columns of the Temple of Poseidon.

Uncle Dorian held his hands together as though he was praying and brought them to his chin. "Yes," he said, after a moment, "but we must wait for Daedalus. He will give us safe passage back."

Maia kicked at the rocky ground, her mind a jumble of thoughts and pictures.

"You know, I met a god."

"Really?"

"And I was almost attacked by a gryphon in the woods."

"Humph."

"Which of these do you think I should tell my mother when she picks me up from the airport tomorrow?"

"I would think neither."

"Yeah," Maia said, as she scooped up a handful of rocks. "She probably wouldn't ever let me come back."

"You would return to Greece?" Uncle Dorian asked, his eyebrows arched in surprise.

Ignoring his question, Maia threw the rocks in the direction of the cliff side where days before, in another place, she'd thrown the bracelet Icarus had given her.

"Yaya must be sick with worry."

"I told your grandmother that we decided to spend a few days visiting the coast."

"With no change of clothes?"

"I assured her I would buy you whatever you needed. Helena was very jealous apparently."

"Yaya doesn't know about—"

"She does not remember," Uncle Dorian said, interrupting Maia's question. "And it is best that it remains so."

"More secrets," Maia mumbled.

"What did you say?"

"When did my life get so full of secrets? A few weeks ago, I thought I knew everything or at least everything that mattered."

"And what is it that matters most to a thirteen-year-old girl?"

Maia hesitated. "I don't know. Family, I guess. While I've been here outrunning bearded sociopaths, my Grandpa's been lying in a hospital bed. My mom works hard – really, really hard. She's been trying to forget my father for years, and all I've been trying to do is learn who he is, even if it meant my mother getting hurt again."

Maia ran her fingers over the bracelet Zeus had given her. "At least now I know the truth."

"You do?"

"He's dead. My father sacrificed his life to keep me and my mother and a whole lot of other people safe."

Maia stared at the Temple of Poseidon, barely acknowledging the look of dismay on Uncle Dorian's face. She searched her memory for some deeper meaning to attach to Poseidon's name.

"You know what I don't get? For weeks leading up to coming to Greece, all I did was read about its history and mythology. But here in Olympia, I can barely remember any of it. I know Poseidon was the god of the sea and a few other things about him, but that's it. It was the same way when I first saw Pierinos, the winged horse. I knew there was a winged horse in some myth, but... I don't know.

It's as if something happens to my memory when I cross over, and the only things I seem to forget have to do with the gods or myths."

"Perhaps it is best."

"Why?"

"Because if you could recall everything you knew about the tales of the gods, you would be too frightened to act."

"Frightened? You mean having some psychotic king order my death wasn't frightening enough?"

Maia twisted her bracelet. "Zeus said this would protect me if I ever wanted to return."

"That was most kind."

"Except that after everything I've experienced here, nothing could make me want to come back. Unless there's something else I don't know."

"Maia, please."

"I know, I know. I shouldn't ask questions if I don't want the answers." Maia paused. "Still, even if I could convince my mother to let me come back to Greece... "

"Your grandmother would happily pay for you to return."

"If I did come back," Maia continued, "I'd want it to be on my terms. I need to get one of those flashbulb things that Icarus's father created."

Uncle Dorian looked skyward. "Speaking of whom... "

From over the Temple of Poseidon came a flurry of white. Daedalus, astride Pierinos, looked down grimly at Maia and Uncle Dorian. Circling around, Pierinos landed a few feet away from Maia. Instantly, the horse reared back, nearly throwing Daedalus.

"Easy, Pierinos, you silly creature."

The horse gave a few more kicks and shakes of its head before settling down. Daedalus ran his hand through Pierinos's mane. "There is nothing to fear."

Maia wondered if his words were meant for her or the horse.

"I see you were able to capture him again," said Uncle Dorian.

"Yes. It happens so often that I have become quite adept at it."

"That and many other things, I would say."

Daedalus eased himself off Pierinos. "Now, where is my son?"

Maia felt a pang of guilt. "He... he didn't make it. His wings were damaged, and he fell into the sea."

To Maia's disbelief, Daedalus appeared unmoved by the news of his son's fate. Coolly, he looked Maia up and down. "You are unhurt?"

Maia shook her head in anger. "Didn't you hear what I said? Icarus fell into the sea! Doesn't that bother you? Aren't you even a little bit upset?"

"Child, you must—"

"No! Icarus may've gotten me into this mess, but he also rescued me. He cared about me, and I... " Maia stopped herself, not knowing how to finish.

"Maia, please try to understand," said Uncle Dorian. "Daedalus will deal with his son's disappearance after he has sent us home."

"I don't believe you people. You're all crazy. I'm never coming back here."

Maia sat on the ground and held her head in her hands. She wished that everything had been a dream, especially for the people that'd been lost. Because of her, Ophelos was dead and Icarus had fallen into the sea. This trip started out being about her father, but somewhere along the way it changed drastically and she was ready for it to end. Maia stood and faced Uncle Dorian and Daedalus.

"Maia, I hope—" Uncle Dorian began.

Maia waved her hand to stop him from continuing. "Please, just take me home."

Pierinos reared back, giving a loud cry.

"Whoa, Pierinos! Whoa!" called Daedalus.

Pierinos continued to rear back, and in one majestic motion the horse took flight.

"Ridiculous creature," grumbled Daedalus. "What could have made it—" His eyes narrowed as he caught sight of Maia's bracelet.

"Where did you get that?"

"It was a gift," Maia answered, staring straight at Daedalus.

"From whom?"

"From someone who thought I might want to come back here one day – on my terms! Now, I'd like to be sent home."

Daedalus kept his eyes fixed on the bracelet. After several seconds, he turned his attention to Uncle Dorian.

"This will complicate matters."

"I do not think now is the time to discuss this," Uncle Dorian replied, his eyes betraying a flicker of anger.

"Fine," said Daedalus, in a tone that signaled to Maia that he was anything but content with this turn of events.

Maia stared at her bracelet, turning her wrist over and back again in an effort to make sense of the pictures.

"You would be well advised to keep that bracelet safe," Daedalus told her.

"Don't worry," Maia answered, "I will. So, am I going—"

"Yes, you are going home... now."

There was a flash of bright light. Maia rubbed her eyes, and, as her vision returned, the Temple of Poseidon loomed before her. Its columns were cracked and fragmented, and it no longer appeared as grand and alluring.

"Just like this whole trip," she muttered.

CHAPTER 26

UNTIL THE NEXT TIME

MAIA SPOKE VERY LITTLE on the drive from Cape Sounion to her grandmother's house. After making several futile attempts to engage her, Uncle Dorian settled on having Maia listen as he recounted the details of their supposed trip up and down the coast, providing a cover if she wanted to speak to anyone in the family about her missing day.

"Maia," Uncle Dorian said, as they pulled up to her grandmother's house, "if there is one thing I can implore you, it is to not tell your grandmother—"

Maia didn't let him finish. She got out of the car and walked into the house. Maia gave her grandmother a hug and headed straight for her bedroom. Maia threw herself on the bed and closed her eyes. She tried to empty her mind of every thought. It took some effort, but eventually she fell asleep.

Maia slept for most of the day. When she did wake up, it was after a particularly nasty dream in which she was being lowered into a dark, rank-smelling pit while several onlookers laughed and cheered. Maia looked at the clock. It was almost evening. Uncle Dorian must have convinced her grandmother to let her sleep. Maia found a plate of fruit, bread, and cheese on the nightstand – left there, she assumed, by her grandmother. She stared at it but realized she had no appetite.

Maia got out of bed and walked to the curtains. Every muscle ached, especially those in her neck and shoulders. She hesitated for a moment, anxious that someone would be waiting for her on the other side, and then pulled the curtains open. The sun was setting over the hills. Maia squinted to see if she could make out a god pulling the sun in a chariot but then turned away, overcome with a wave of regret. She should've believed Icarus sooner.

Her bracelet glinted in the light of the setting sun. Maia rubbed it with her other hand, taking comfort in the words of Zeus. The bracelet would keep her safe. Looking at it again, Maia drew back. She twisted the bracelet several times but finally accepted that all of the symbols had disappeared – except for one. Maia hadn't noticed it before. It was a pair of wings.

Maia closed the curtains and walked over to the bedroom door. There were voices coming from the living room. Maia considered going back to sleep but winced as she remembered her dream. Maia heard a bell ring, and she groaned at the thought of members of her extended family arriving to say goodbye. The bell rang again, and Maia realized it wasn't a doorbell but the telephone. She'd forgotten that her mother had said she'd be calling.

Maia flung open the door and ran down the hallway. Stepping into the light of her grandmother's living room, Maia heard Uncle Dorian's voice coming from the kitchen.

"Yes, she is fine. She is sleeping. I am afraid we have kept her very busy."

"I'm here!" Maia said, entering the kitchen.

"Oh, wait a moment. She is awake and very excited to speak to you. Thank you. Goodbye."

Maia grabbed the telephone. "Mom!"

"Maia, sweetie, it's so good to hear your voice. I have wonderful news! Grandpa woke up last night. He's talking and eating, and he keeps asking for you."

Maia's eyes filled with tears. She didn't understand how, but Zeus had kept his promise.

"Mom, tell Grandpa I can't wait to see him. I have so much I want him to hear."

"So, it sounds like you're ready to come home?"

Maia paused. Was she ready? She wasn't sure of the answer.

"Yeah, I guess I am," Maia said, "but do you think I could come back one day?"

Maia's mother laughed. "We can talk about that once you're home."

Maia and her mother spoke for a few more minutes about the details of her return flight and where in the airport she was to meet Adriana. Her mother repeated the information several times, but after everything Maia had experienced in Olympia, she didn't object at all to being mothered.

"Okay, Mom. I love you."

"I love you too, Maia. I'll see you tomorrow."

After hanging up the telephone, Maia found herself facing her grandmother and Uncle Dorian as they sat at the kitchen table. "Um, I think I'll go back to bed," Maia said, feeling awkward and self-conscious.

Maia's grandmother said something in Greek to her uncle, an unmistakable look of worry on her face.

"Your grandmother is concerned that you have not eaten."

"I'll eat what was left in my room. I'm just so tired." Maia smiled at her grandmother to show that she appreciated her concern.

Her grandmother smiled in return, stood up, and grasped Maia's hand. "Grandmother miss you."

"I'm going to miss you too," Maia said, her voice cracking.

Her grandmother started to cry. She let go of Maia's hand and pulled a handkerchief from a pocket in the front of her apron. Wiping her eyes, Maia's grandmother attempted another smile.

"You come back?"

"Yes," Maia answered, realizing how much she really did want to come back. "I hope so," she added.

Uncle Dorian spoke to Maia's grandmother in Greek, and the older woman nodded in response.

"Your grandmother wants to give you something. She does not want to go to the airport tomorrow. She is afraid it will be too emotional."

Maia's grandmother slapped Uncle Dorian's arm and said something in a scolding tone. Uncle Dorian rolled his eyes. "She did not want me to tell you that."

Maia's grandmother shuffled to the counter and pulled a small package out of a drawer.

"To remember," she said, handing the package to Maia.

Maia unwrapped the package with great care. Inside was a small, plastic jewelry box. Maia looked up at her grandmother and smiled. She pulled off the lid of the box and found a silver coin on a chain necklace inside.

"You like?"

"Very much," Maia said, as she hugged her grandmother. "It's wonderful."

* * *

MAIA SPENT THE NEXT MORNING packing her suitcase before walking into town with Helena for some last-minute souvenir buying. Maia almost bought her grandfather a lighter but thought better of the idea. Instead, she bought him a leather money clip with the flag of Greece on it. Maia found a shirt for her mother – the same style of which she remembered her mother wearing in the pictures in her grandmother's house. Helena teased Maia, saying she should buy one for herself to attract boys back home, but Maia was drawn to a small, metal sculpture of a winged horse. Maia thought it would have to suffice until the next time, if there was indeed a next time, she was able to ride Pierinos again.

Walking back to her grandmother's house, Maia tried to piece together everything she'd experienced. Clearly, her trip to Greece had turned out nothing like she thought it would. She was leaving with more questions than she'd had when she arrived.

"Why do you look so serious?" Helena asked.

Maia thought a bit. "Did you ever feel like you didn't know who you were?"

Helena stopped and gave Maia a long, hard look. It was unlike any expression Maia had seen on her cousin's face. For a moment, she thought Helena had something important to reveal. Perhaps she did know about Olympia.

"Sometimes," Helena admitted, "but then I think, I have time. Until then, I will have fun."

Maia wondered if she'd ever feel that carefree again.

CHAPTER 27

FOR ANOTHER DAY

ADRIANA STOPPED CRYING five hours into the flight home.

"I don't understand," she said, between short, agonizing breaths, "why he doesn't even want to try to make things work. Who cares if he lives in Chicago? We had such an amazing week together."

Maia listened with as much sympathy as she could muster as Adriana relayed, in excruciating detail, how the boy in the wool cap Maia had seen at the airport when they arrived had broken Adriana's heart after a weeklong, whirlwind romance. Adriana had even considered applying to Northwestern University to be closer to him.

"Maia, I hope you'll never know what it's like to go through this," Adriana told her. "Boys cause nothing but heartbreak."

Maia looked at the pair of wings on her bracelet.

"Some boys are okay."

* * *

AS MAIA WALKED PAST the customs station in the airport in New York, she wondered if her mother was going to notice anything different about her – if her experiences in Olympia had changed her somehow. She approached the set of sliding glass doors that separated her from the main lobby of the terminal. The effort it took to cross the threshold felt almost as great as flying.

181

* * *

SITTING IN MEMORIAL PARK, Maia marveled at how odd it was that her life, for the most part, was normal again. In the weeks since she'd left Greece, the repairs to her house had all been finished. And Grandpa was back to his old self with one major exception – he'd sworn off smoking forever. When he returned home from the hospital, Maia would keep him company on their front steps. He wanted Maia to tell him about every second of her trip, and she obliged him, filling in fake details where necessary. She spent many a cool evening on her front steps this way, even practicing her guitar a few times.

Maia's mother was as busy with work as ever, but Maia noticed a subtle change in her too. Despite everything they'd been through over the summer, she seemed more optimistic, and Maia even caught her mother humming a tune a few times, something she'd rarely done before.

The biggest surprise had come the day Maia spotted her mother's car while she was walking to the library. It was parked at the end of Sea Cliff Avenue across from Memorial Park. Her mother had told Maia she'd be working late, but instead she was in the park, sitting on the same bench Maia loved and staring out at the harbor. Maia had watched her mother for a few minutes and then, not wanting to intrude, allowed her mother her privacy. Maia had walked back home and waited for her mother on the front steps with her guitar. Fifteen minutes later, Maia's mother pulled up in front of their house. Her face brightened when she saw Maia.

"I thought you had to work late," Maia said.

"I gave up the shift to someone else. Let's get Grandpa and go out," her mother said. "I'm starving, and I bet you could use some new picks for that guitar."

* * *

LOOKING OUT AT THE HARBOR, Maia thought about the poem she'd had to analyze on her English final so many weeks ago. Maia had never liked poetry, but this poem kept popping up in her head, especially since her trip to Greece – one line in particular.

"I'd rather be a pagan... "

Maia looked at her bracelet – her gift from Zeus. She hadn't taken it or the necklace her grandmother had given her off since returning home. Maia ran her fingers over the bracelet.

"In case I ever want to go back... " she whispered.

It was a possibility Maia would put off considering for another day.

* * *

TRITON WATCHED THE GIRL sitting on the bench.

How little does she understand.

The sea god had completed the mandate given to him. He'd ensured that the girl made it home safely. His task accomplished, Triton prepared for the journey home, displeased by the prospect of traveling through those dirty waters.

Perhaps I shall sink a few of their ships. That should teach them to start respecting this realm once again.

The sea god gave a parting glance to the girl. She was content.

Enjoy your quietude, child of two worlds. May it endure... as long as the gods allow.

MAIA'S ADVENTURES
IN OLYMPIA CONTINUE...

Three years after discovering a startling truth about her heritage, Maia Peterson thought it was safe to return to Olympia – a hidden world of fearsome giants, enchanting nymphs, and other creatures and characters from Greek mythology – if she wore the magic bracelet given to her by Zeus, lord of the gods. But when the queen of the Amazons, a tribe of powerful warrior women, falls prey to a mad, bloodthirsty demigod, Maia risks Zeus's protection to fulfill a promise once made by her long-missing father.

Side by side with the mightiest of combatants, Maia is pitted against an old rival who wants nothing more than to see her fall in battle – all under the watchful eye of forces that hold her to be the key to the future of Olympia... and the world she calls home.

MAIA *and* HIPPOLYTA

For more information, visit:
barrowcourtbooks.com

ACKNOWLEDGMENTS

MY SINCERE THANKS to everyone who championed early drafts of *Maia and Icarus*, and especially to my editor, Beverly Ehrman, for her insight and advice; to my illustrator, Peter Prabowo, for bringing Maia and her world to life so beautifully; to my art director and designer, Michael Ebert, for his expert craftsmanship and counsel; to Andie Ebert, for her unfailing enthusiasm and encouragement; and to Eric Rubin, for setting me on my own epic journey.

ABOUT *the* AUTHOR

JAMES A. PEREZ has worked in the field of education for over twenty years with children of all ages. He is a proud husband, father, and lifelong comic book fan who lives on Long Island with his family – including his niece, Maia. Born of his love of Greek mythology, this is his first book.

CPSIA information can be obtained
at www.ICGtesting.com
Printed in the USA
LVHW040023270522
719852LV00001B/209

9 780989 176224